The Lyon's Redemption

The Lyon's Den Connected World

Sandra Sookoo

© Copyright 2023 by Sandra Sookoo
Text by Sandra Sookoo
Cover by Dar Albert

Dragonblade Publishing, Inc. is an imprint of Kathryn Le Veque Novels, Inc.
P.O. Box 23
Moreno Valley, CA 92556
ceo@dragonbladepublishing.com

Produced in the United States of America

First Edition October 2023
Print Edition

Reproduction of any kind except where it pertains to short quotes in relation to advertising or promotion is strictly prohibited.

All Rights Reserved.

The characters and events portrayed in this book are fictitious. Any similarity to real persons, living or dead, is purely coincidental and not intended by the author.

ARE YOU SIGNED UP FOR DRAGONBLADE'S BLOG?

You'll get the latest news and information on exclusive giveaways, exclusive excerpts, coming releases, sales, free books, cover reveals and more.

Check out our complete list of authors, too!

No spam, no junk. That's a promise!

Sign Up Here

www.dragonbladepublishing.com

Dearest Reader;

Thank you for your support of a small press. At Dragonblade Publishing, we strive to bring you the highest quality Historical Romance from some of the best authors in the business. Without your support, there is no 'us', so we sincerely hope you adore these stories and find some new favorite authors along the way.

Happy Reading!

CEO, Dragonblade Publishing

Additional Dragonblade books by Author Sandra Sookoo

Willful Winterbournes Series
Romancing Miss Quill (Book 1)
Pursuing Mr. Mattingly (Book 2)
Courting Lady Yeardly (Book 3)
Guarding the Widow Pellingham (Book 4)
Bedeviling Major Kenton (Book 5)
Charming Miss Standish (Book 6)
Teasing Miss Atherby (Novella)

The Storme Brother Series
The Soul of a Storme (Book 1)
The Heart of a Storme (Book 2)
The Look of a Storme (Book 3)
A Storme's Christmas Legacy
A Storme's First Noelle
The Sting of a Storme (Book 4)
The Touch of a Storme (Book 5)
The Fury of a Storme (Book 6)
Much Ado About a Storme (in the *A Duke in Winter* anthology)

The Lyon's Den Series
The Lyon's Puzzle
The Lyon's Redemption

Other Lyon's Den Books

Into the Lyon's Den by Jade Lee
The Scandalous Lyon by Maggi Andersen
Fed to the Lyon by Mary Lancaster
The Lyon's Lady Love by Alexa Aston
The Lyon's Laird by Hildie McQueen
The Lyon Sleeps Tonight by Elizabeth Ellen Carter
A Lyon in Her Bed by Amanda Mariel
Fall of the Lyon by Chasity Bowlin
Lyon's Prey by Anna St. Claire
Loved by the Lyon by Collette Cameron
The Lyon's Den in Winter by Whitney Blake
Kiss of the Lyon by Meara Platt
Always the Lyon Tamer by Emily E K Murdoch
To Tame the Lyon by Sky Purington
How to Steal a Lyon's Fortune by Alanna Lucas
The Lyon's Surprise by Meara Platt
A Lyon's Pride by Emily Royal
Lyon Eyes by Lynne Connolly
Tamed by the Lyon by Chasity Bowlin
Lyon Hearted by Jade Lee
The Devilish Lyon by Charlotte Wren
Lyon in the Rough by Meara Platt
Lady Luck and the Lyon by Chasity Bowlin
Rescued by the Lyon by C.H. Admirand
Pretty Little Lyon by Katherine Bone
The Courage of a Lyon by Linda Rae Sande
Pride of Lyons by Jenna Jaxon
The Lyon's Share by Cerise DeLand
The Heart of a Lyon by Anna St. Claire

Into the Lyon of Fire by Abigail Bridges
Lyon of the Highlands by Emily Royal
The Lyon's Puzzle by Sandra Sookoo
Lyon at the Altar by Lily Harlem
Captivated by the Lyon by C.H. Admirand
The Lyon's Secret by Laura Trentham
The Talons of a Lyon by Jude Knight
The Lyon and the Lamb by Elizabeth Keysian
To Claim a Lyon's Heart by Sherry Ewing
A Lyon of Her Own by Anna St. Claire
Don't Wake a Sleeping Lyon by Sara Adrien
The Lyon and the Bluestocking by E.L. Johnson
The Lyon's Perfect Mate by Cerise DeLand
The Lyon Who Loved Me by Tracy Sumner
Lyon of the Ton by Emily Royal
Truth or Lyon by Katherine Bone

Dedication

To Kristina Stevens. I'm so glad you love my books and let yourself get lost amidst their pages when you need a break from reality. Thanks for the encouraging words and continuing support. It means a lot.

Author's Note

Though this is a romance, some of the subject matter discussed herein is of a sensitive nature and deals with stillbirth/miscarriage/pregnancy loss. If you are sensitive to this or triggered by seeing it discussed as part of the healing process, please be advised it is a continuous thread that moves throughout the book.

Chapter One

December 15, 1817
The Lyon's Den
London, England

*H*ELL'S BELLS. W*ILL this ghastly anniversary not pass quickly?*
This was the most distasteful day—as it always was—and for the last seven damned years, he'd been forced to live through it and the memories that it brought.

With a huff of annoyance, Thomas Prestwick—Viscount of Ashbury—sent his glance around the smoking lounge of the Lyon's Den gambling hell, then took a large sip of his brandy. A handful of men had gathered in here as a sort of refuge from the activities on the main gaming floor, to either gather their courage to continue, or realize their losses were so heavy this night that they had no choice but to return home or attempt to console themselves with one of the courtesans provided by the Lyon's Den.

Either way, it was a disturbing and perhaps sad commentary on the state of the lives of bored men within the *ton*.

To that end, how the hell had it become December? Wasn't it just yesterday he was at this very club, teasing his best friend Pennington about being unexpectedly matched by the mysterious owner of the gaming hell, Mrs. Dove-Lyon? Damn, but that had been almost two months prior, and the earl was due to return to Town from a quick wedding trip in Brighton. Why the devil the pair had wanted to travel there when it was far too cold to enjoy the seaside, he would never know, but then, love was like a maggot in the brain and removed a man's common sense.

Poor bastard.

He huffed again and took another sip of the rather fine brandy. Whatever else Mrs. Dove-Lyon was, she somehow managed to stock the Lyon's Den with the absolute best of everything, but damn. Not even the first-rate liquor could remove the ennui he suffered as well at the guilt that had become stifling as of late.

The bloody Christmastide holidays would soon be upon them, and those merry strings of days only exacerbated the fact he was alone. Christ, but he despised any excuse for families to gather, to endure assemblies full of laughter and cheer and fragrant fir boughs when he had left all of it behind long ago by a simple twist of fate.

Seven years ago this very day, the love of his life had perished after laboring to bring their daughter into the world. He'd loved Cynthia, loved her as fiercely and completely as only a man of nine and twenty could, for he'd never been in love before that time. She'd been barely nineteen, fresh-faced and new to Town. The position in the Prestwick household had been her first, her parents had been tenants on his father's estate in the Essex countryside, but *his* father had been violently opposed to the match. Thomas was the heir to a viscounty, and she had been naught but a chambermaid.

The love wasn't sanctioned, and neither was it tolerated. While it was perfectly acceptable for the son of a viscount to get off his rocks with a servant, he was absolutely never in any circumstance to marry one. It had been a bitter pill to swallow. However, their love had burned bright despite the opposition and the obstacles littering their path. There had been a certain addiction to that forbidden relationship and how they had been forced to sneak about whenever they wanted to meet, but Cynthia was a beautiful girl, so dainty and blonde and perfect except for her pedigree.

Or lack thereof.

After a few months, he'd asked her to marry him; it was all very hushed and clandestine, for he'd wanted time to gather the courage to tell his father. They'd planned to do the deed while at his father's country estate, for Cynthia was increasing and it was growing too difficult to continue hiding the fact, but then tragedy struck before the Christmastide trip could be made. The babe came earlier than expected, which threw the whole Prestwick household into chaos. Secrets had come out, shame had been measured, parental anger had landed upon his head. Threats were issued that Thomas would be disowned if he persisted with his foolish plans.

In the end, it hadn't mattered, for Cynthia had perished giving birth, and when it became evident there was something… different about the child—a flattened face, especially the bridge of the nose, almond-shaped eyes that slanted upward, a rather slower response time and sluggish movements—Thomas had the decision of his life to make. He'd known the signs; how could he not? His own brother had had those same traits, and though he was only three years Thomas' junior, he'd been sent away, boarded out to various families throughout Essex until he'd died of natural causes perhaps ten years ago.

The horror of those days had come rushing back. Should he keep the child, raise it as his own and thereby give credence to the tales swirling wildly about, or should he follow the dictates of his father, who had ordered the child be put into an orphanage immediately?

There truly was no recourse, never had been. The baby girl was bundled up with her mother a few hours dead and was sent away. Thomas was then given a dressing down that had his ears ringing all these years later.

To his father's credit, the man had given coin to the institution where the child was sent as well as a modest payment to the maid's mother—her father had died years before—as a way to wash his hands of the affair. Just like that, the indiscretion was swept tidily beneath the proverbial rug and neither of them had spoken of it again.

But Thomas remembered. Good God how he remembered, for that time had left a jagged hole in his heart that nothing had been able to heal or even repair.

Perhaps he was beyond that. He had responsibilities, and as the years marched on, he needed to attend them.

Now that he held the title of viscount following his father's death two years before, he was beginning to see that whole episode from his sire's point of view. He—Thomas—had been completely irresponsible, hadn't given thought to his future or the reputation of the title, had committed the unforgiveable crime of giving his heart to a servant. He'd thrown his upbringing away in order to chase after something that probably wouldn't have had a chance in hell of maturing.

And still the guilt remained. It burned in the center of his chest, left his gut churning year after year, especially once Christmastide came calling and he wondered what it might be like if he had been fortunate enough to have a wife, a child, a family to share his life with.

Directly following his father's death, he had located the girl—named Sally; he'd asked the adoptive family to grant him that tiny honor—and had made certain she had been placed with an adoptive family who would be good to her. Of course, the annual payments he gave the couple had helped with that encouragement, and though he could sleep more soundly knowing the girl wouldn't rot away unwanted in an orphanage, that act of kindness hadn't lessened the guilt or displaced the regret.

"Of all the places to hide while in a brown study."

The sound of his friend's voice brought his head around with a frown. As Captain Simon Henry Huxley came closer with a cheroot in hand and a snifter of brandy in the other, Thomas relaxed slightly and welcomed him with a tight grin. "Fancy seeing your sorry arse here."

"I had nothing else to do tonight." He sat his lean form in the leather chair that matched the one Thomas occupied.

A captain in the Navy during his salad days, an injury forced his retirement, but the black leather eyepatch over his left eye only made him that more dashing. Dressed in the first stare of fashion, his black hair had been arranged in a popular style, his collar points just so, the folds of his starched cravat artistically balanced, it was said he'd rather be caught dead then appear in public with even a hair ruffled. The captain enjoyed everything in order, and everything had a place—including the people in his life—but beyond that rigidness, he was kind and caring, a benevolent landowner of some impressive fortune, which made him a favorite as he hobnobbed with the nobility in the *ton*. They had been close friends for more years than Thomas could count.

"Somehow, I find that difficult to believe. Everyone reserves a piece of your time."

Simon snorted. Amusement danced in his sapphire-hued eye. "A large part of being successful in this life is the connections one makes, so I gladly do the circuit while in London, because if furthers my own causes." He took a drag on the cheroot and then blew out a perfect smoke ring toward the ceiling. "And I do so enjoy relieving lesser men of their coin at the tables here at the Lyon's Den."

"Now that rings with truth." Thomas finished the remainder of his brandy in one gulp and welcomed the sting of the liquor in his throat.

"What are your plans for the night? You have been moping since Pennington's nuptials."

Thomas rolled his eyes to the smoke-shrouded ceiling. "I *do* have other friends and interests in London outside of him, you know." Though things were rather dull just now, with a good portion of

London's most exciting residents dispersed to their country estates for the damned holiday.

"Then perhaps you and I should go out on the floor or do a few rounds of private wagering. Collecting an easy windfall before Christmas would prove most helpful in obtaining luxuries we've all been deprived off after last year's horrid weather."

"God, yes, last year was a disaster." Crops failed due to the constant rain and cold temperatures and in some places in England, snow even in the summer. It would take a few years to recover from the lost income, which was why men like him haunted gaming hells like this one—easy coin especially if men with little skill were drunk at the tables. "Will faro hold my attention, though?"

"It's a good sight better than sulking here for whatever reason."

Even though the captain and Pennington were his closest friends, he had never shared the whole debacle of Cynthia or the child with them, for he'd been embarrassed and hurt and quite frankly, talking about it still made him unreasonably angry.

"I am *not* sulking."

"Scowling into the smoke then," the captain said with a grin that no doubt won him countless bed partners.

"Not scowling. Reflecting, perhaps."

"Ha!" Simon swallowed the remainder of his brandy in one gulp. After resting the glass on a small table at his elbow, he snuffed out the cheroot into the glass then trained his full attention on Thomas. "Too much thinking is bad for a man. Makes you soft. Or insane." He tapped his temple with a forefinger. "Perhaps you should marry. It has made a world of difference with Pennington. He is actually quite pleasant to be around now, and it seems as if his mental... worries have lessened somewhat."

"Marriage. Perish the thought." As a younger man, he'd wanted that life. Now, he disdained it. Love and romance were not sustainable, and they were merely an illusion. "Parson's mousetrap is not my path."

Not anymore.

"Yet you have a responsibility to your title, to at least secure the line in the event you kick off this mortal coil."

As if I needed that grim reminder. "I don't want that either." The fact of the matter was he remained conflicted on what he *did* want from life. "Until then, I'll languish here and indulge in as many sins as I can find."

Until I can forget… everything.

Not that it had helped for the past handful of years.

For long moments, they sat in silence. Then Simon leaned toward him and said in a low voice, "So then you'll continue to draw your political caricatures and submit them anonymously to poke fun at everyone who stokes your ire?"

Heat crept up the back of his neck. "You are the only one who knows about that," he hissed with a furtive glance about the area, but no one paid them much mind. "But yes. It is the one thing that gives me joy."

A few years ago, the doodles and sarcastic drawings he used to do to pass the time had caught the eye of a newspaper editor when they'd both been at the same club one evening. After a brief talk over brandy and a losing hand of cards on the editor's account, Thomas was offered a position of having his drawings published in a few papers every other week.

They ended up both humoring and inflaming the general public, which made a tidy side income for him, and would for as long as he could remain anonymous.

"Perhaps you should make one of yourself. It might yank you from the doldrums," Simon said in all seriousness.

"Do shut up." Christ, but it would prove a long night if his friend persisted in badgering him. He launched himself from the comfortable leather chair. "Let's go onto the gaming floor. I'm not of a mind to talk, nor do I wish to spend the night with a courtesan upstairs."

Though he'd made use of the brothel at the Lyon's Den many times before, the urge simply wasn't there tonight.

Perhaps Simon was right, and he wished to sulk.

Bah! Damned Christmastide season.

"Excellent choice." Though the other man eyed him with suspicion, he stood as well. "We are fair enough gamblers that this should be a relatively easy night."

"Indeed." Though neither of them had the skill that Pennington did, they weren't exactly horrid. But the earl's absence only served to remind him that he would spend Christmas night with his best friend, sitting about his dinner table and having a firsthand witness to new love. Of course, there was always the possibility the man might wish to remove to the country for his first Christmas as a married man. Considerably cheered by that thought, Thomas grinned. "Perhaps we shall amass a fortune tonight, eh, Captain?"

"We can only hope. It's damned expensive living in London."

No doubt it was for a man who hadn't been born to wealth, but then, that was Simon's path, not his. As soon as they stepped into the gaming hall, the general mood in the air shifted to one of excitement, anxiety, and despair. The sounds of crystal clinking against crystal echoed, punctuated by cries of victory as well as defeat. Low purrs of laughter came from various courtesans circling the room looking for their next partner and spurring the fortunate on at the tables. At the opposite side of the room, the more soothing sounds of a string quartet played music fit for a stage, for it wouldn't do to have the gamblers enraged from losses Thomas suspected were designed—a time or two—to put the house at full advantage.

Still, his heartbeat accelerated, and he couldn't wait to find a spot at one of the tables. There was a certain feeling of being alive when one was embroiled in wagering.

"What is your pleasure tonight, Ashbury?"

"I'm not entirely sure." Another glance about the space had anticipation sailing down his spine. He might utilize the gaming hell more than he properly should, but what else was there in Town to hold his attention and keep him from letting loose the emotions and hurt he'd kept back over the years?

When he glanced up at the second floor, he caught sight of the owner, Mrs. Dove-Lyon, prowling the ladies' gallery. She was the most mysterious person he'd ever laid eyes on, and tonight was no exception as she trailed veils and skirting that made her resemble a spirit more than anything else. Did anyone truly know what she looked like? He rather doubted it. Every so often she would peer downward, and when her gaze happened to crash into his, a sudden chill went through him.

Before he could wonder if that stare meant she'd singled him out this night, he dismissed her from his mind. It was merely a ploy to see him—as well as the other men wagering here tonight—rattled enough to falter at the tables. More losses meant more coin she took in that would line her own pockets. However, the rumors that she mucked about in people's lives and played at being a matchmaker between titled, rich men and troublesome, scandal-ridden women of the *ton* couldn't be denied. After all, that was what happened to Pennington.

The chill passed, and Simon nudged him in the ribs with an elbow. "Interesting woman, Mrs. Dove-Lyon. Perhaps you should plead your case with her. That would be the ultimate gamble, hmm? Letting her arrange a match?"

"For her price and bother? No thank you." Nothing the woman did would come cheap. "If I were a marriage-minded lord, I certainly wouldn't take a woman trailing scandal and drama in her wake. Has the potential to be a love match."

"Ah, that makes sense since your reputation within the *ton* is so sterling." Heavy sarcasm hung on the words.

The corners of Thomas' lips twitched with the urge to chuckle. Perhaps he needed this night with his friend after all. "No, because I have had my fill of both of those things and never wish to go through them again."

Simon snorted in amusement. "Scandal or love?"

"Exactly." Never again. If that meant he would be alone for the remainder of his life, so be it. The title could pass to a distant relative for all he cared.

The captain shook his head. "Let us indulge in faro then, else I'll wager with some of the men here at how long it will take you to cast up your accounts when you fall into your cups."

"That will not happen." He shook his head and looked askance at his friend as they joined a table. "I refuse to drink when I wager. I want a clear head." Two other men were seated at the table. One was an older gentleman with salt-and-pepper hair while the other was around Thomas' age with red hair that gleamed like fire beneath the chandeliers.

"Fair enough." Simon nodded in welcome at the dealer. "We would like to join."

The dealer nodded. "Of course." The man glanced a question to one of the high-ranking representatives who worked directly beneath Mrs. Dove-Lyon, for every man in this lofty position often circulated through the rooms to keep an eye on the guests within. Mr. Vance wasn't easy on the eyes, but he had sharp business acumen and a sharper wit. He made certain to toss out men in dun territory or with pockets to let, as well as the occasional man who mistreated the courtesans. When Mr. Vance gave an imperceptible nod, the dealer, dressed in black, glanced at him with a faint grin. "It's a fifty-thousand pound buy-in, Captain Huxley, Lord Ashbury."

Damn. Games at the Lyon's Den were not for the faint at heart.

Mr. Vance raised a dark eyebrow and crossed his massive arms across his chest as if he doubted either of them had the blunt.

Thomas narrowed his eyes. He might not be worth as much as a duke or earl, but the contents of his coffers were nothing to sneeze at.

Though, he would need a few wins tonight to make certain he had a cushion. "Easily covered. My credit is good here else you wouldn't have let me in." He glanced at Simon. "What of you?" There was no knowing the state of the captain's finances.

Huxley shrugged. "I am in for one game." He looked at the dealer. "Proceed."

As faro began, Thomas lightly conversed with Simon. Fortune at cards was presenting confidence that intimidated one's opponents. Card after card was presented and bets placed. Wager after wager fell, but Thomas won most, with a few gains going in Simon's favor. Eventually, the older gentleman bowed out with his apologies, while the red-haired man struggled. Obviously, he had no skill in the game. It was only a matter of time before he lost handily.

By the time the deck was exhausted, and another handful of wagers were placed, Thomas had increased his initial deposit by two while Simon made back his buy-in.

Then the dynamic at the table shifted.

The red-haired man tugged on the knot of his cravat. "I apologize, Lord Ashbury, but I am unable to cover this loss." A sheen of sweat appeared on his upper lip, while horror dawned in his dark gray eyes.

Mr. Vance took a step toward the table.

"However," the man held up a hand, palm outward that halted the burly man's movements, "I can offer you the hand of my sister in exchange for wiping clean my debt."

From beside him, Simon snorted. "Whatever will you do, I wonder?" he asked in a low whisper heavy with amusement.

"What the devil is this? What use have I for a woman, sight unseen?" Thomas narrowed his eyes on the man as knots of warning pulled in his gut. "I'd rather have your payment."

The dealer frowned and stared at Thomas. "It is your choice, Lord Ashbury. What is your answer to Mr. Jameson?"

"I—" Before he could decide, the red-haired man rushed onward.

"I haven't the funds, you see." His cheeks and neck were as red as his hair. "I knew I shouldn't have wagered so heavily, but it was great fun, and I thought I could rout you."

Mr. Vance approached the table. "Shall I go upstairs and ask Mrs. Dove-Lyon's opinion? You have my apologies for allowing such a person through the door, Lord Ashbury."

"Think nothing of it. Some men are better liars than others." He glared at the hapless Mr. Jameson. "I will wait on the ruling from her."

While Mr. Vance went off with the dealer, Thomas crossed his arms at his chest and rested his stare on Mr. Jameson. The name seemed slightly familiar, but he couldn't immediately place it. "Why are you here tonight?"

The man shrugged. "I needed a quick influx of coin. Times have been rough, and after last year, being an importer of fine goods hasn't made the income it should." He bounced his gaze between Thomas and Simon. "Don't discount my sister, my lord. She's no slouch in looks or temperament."

That meant she was troublesome, and he no doubt wanted her off his hands. "I am not in the market for a wife."

Eventually, the towering Mr. Vance returned. The dealer did not, which meant the game wouldn't be continued. "Mrs. Dove-Lyon has determined Mr. Jameson's sister is as valid as coin." The ghost of a grin graced the big man's lips. "Congratulations, Lord Ashbury. It seems you have won a bride."

"What of me? I do not want to marry, and certainly not in this underhanded way." He didn't trust the expression of relief on Mr. Jameson's face, and he loathed the merry chuckle that sailed from Simon's throat.

"That is the nature of the Lyon's Den. Anything can be wagered. Either you accept what has been offered as payment, or your privileges will be suspended for six months."

"I don't *need* membership here."

"I am sure you do not, but Mrs. Dove-Lyon directed me to also tell you that if you don't accept the offering, she will happily reveal the secret you keep to those in political power." Mr. Vance shrugged. "And that could ruin the rest of your reputation and make life properly difficult for you throughout the *beau monde*."

Damn it all to hell. Of course she knew of his political caricature drawings. The woman knew everything. She must have spies all over London. He shifted in his chair as rage welled up in a hot tide in his chest. Perhaps he could draw out the engagement until the woman asked to be released. "Fine. I accept the modified payment." No one escaped the gaming hell without scratches and scars.

"Very good, my lord." Mr. Vance then stared at Mr. Jameson. "If you will please come with me? Mrs. Dove-Lyon would like a word."

"Of course." Mr. Jameson's face lost all color, but he left the room with the larger man.

"Bah!" Irritated and fuming against Mrs. Dove-Lyon's highhandedness, Thomas tossed his remaining cards upon the table and pushed back his chair with such force it toppled to the polished hardwood floor. "I refuse to wait here for punishment like a boy out of favor with his teacher at school."

"I don't think you have a choice," the captain said with a quick glance about the room. "Her emissary returns."

Then Mr. Vance was there, hulking dark harbinger of doom. "Lord Ashbury, if you will come with me? There are contracts you'll need to sign in Mrs. Dove-Lyon's presence, and terms to discuss with Mr. Jameson in front of the Lyon's Den in-house solicitor."

"All of that can wait until later this week at *my* townhouse with *my* man-of-affairs." He refused to be coerced.

"It cannot, unfortunately," Mr. Vance said with that damned ubiquitous grin. "Mrs. Dove-Lyon retains the right to make certain such things are done properly. When you became a member, you signed paperwork to that effect."

"Of course I did." Thomas cast a glance to Simon, who shrugged. There was nothing he could do. All wagers and results were final at the Lyon's Den. "I may as well hear my sentence, then."

But he would *not* give away his heart in this forced union. Never again would he allow a woman that close, for love was naught but contrived entertainment for those who adored reading such drivel in fairy stories.

Love wasn't real and it certainly could not be found born out of a wager at a gaming table.

Chapter Two

December 16, 1817
Jameson House
Hanover Square
London, England

Miss Olivia Rose Jameson was not best pleased with her brother. For the past day, he'd been uncommonly out of character, jumping at the slightest of noises, tucking himself away in his study to meticulously go over the accounts, keeping out of her company for the most part.

Truly, it didn't matter much to her, for she had much to occupy her thoughts. Yesterday, she had seen a tiny note in one of the newspapers that mentioned the one man in all of England she despised with a burning hot passion. It seemed that Viscount Ashbury would be married soon. Just thinking his title in her mind had her cheeks burning with anger and her chest heating. The man was truly a plague with his tripping through London, indulging in vices as if nothing in his past had mattered.

Well, it mattered to *her*, for he had killed her best friend. They had become such years ago when Cynthia had been a maid in the manor house on the property that neighbored her father's. When they'd discovered an easy and fast friendship, class divide hadn't mattered. They'd connected on a different level, and soon were in each other's pockets as much as they could be during those days.

Eventually, the viscount had destroyed poor Cynthia's life, and in turn, had pulled a pall over hers. With that loss, she'd been plunged into a dark place, for she detested mourning as much as she hated the viscount. It hadn't mattered that Cynthia had been a maid in his household; it hadn't mattered that her head had been turned by his charm and good looks. What mattered was he'd no doubt coerced her into his bed. How she'd died remained a mystery, but she knew he'd been behind it.

So that he could gallivant about London with Cynthia completely forgotten. How many others had he done the same to? How many other lives had he destroyed due to his privilege and attitude of thinking he could take what he wanted?

Well, Olivia refused to let him marry some heiress or an earl's daughter or whomever without being held accountable for what he'd done. For the past seven years, she had bided her time with revenge uppermost in her mind. Perhaps now was the time to enact it, for she was in London and so was he. And with Christmastide nearly upon them, it would be far too easy to encounter him at a society event where she could make nice and merry, flirt her way into his circle, and then either cut him with her dagger or slip enough poison into his drink to make him rue the day he'd ever trifled with her friend. The whole sordid affair had been hushed up with coin spread about to make people at the center of the scandal forget.

Not her. She put Cynthia's face in her mind every morning upon waking so she wouldn't forget... or forgive... the man responsible.

Olivia hadn't quite decided on how she'd get her revenge on him, for she wasn't entirely certain she could kill a man so that he was completely dead. Mostly dead, perhaps. It just depended on the situation, but she was stealthy enough that she wouldn't be caught and skilled enough that she wouldn't falter.

Her father, bless his dead soul, had seen to that. He had made sure she knew how to defend herself, for he'd not trusted anyone since leaving Ireland as a boy. For good reason, but she had no time to let herself remember his old stories.

Tracking down her brother and demanding to know why he was avoiding her was first on her agenda for the day.

"Come, Kip," she softly crooned to her dog as she left her bedroom.

With a yap of delight, the red-gold Pomeranian launched himself from the stack of blankets where he slept and padded quickly to her location. With his fluffy fur, his pointed nose, his dark chocolate eyes, and black whiskers, he was every inch the adorable companion she'd desperately needed after Cynthia's death. In fact, it was from her parents that she'd secured the dog, for they made a nice little side income by breeding the canines.

And it was a personal joke that she'd named the dog Sir Kippington-Prestwick, after the detested Viscount of Ashbury in the hopes that if she were ever fortunate enough to come upon him in the street while walking said dog, she could tell him she'd thought so little of him that she'd named a dog—a fluffy, frou-frou dog—after him.

Quickly, she gained the stairs and took them rather faster than she should, but there was no need for decorum when she was alone in the house with her brother. "Conor? Where are you?" What had prompted him to hide away as if he were suddenly frightened of her? Though she was eight and twenty and he her senior by five years, they had enjoyed a happy childhood and had grown up far away from London in the Essex countryside.

Where her father's acreage had neighbored the viscount's country estate, and all the trouble had begun.

Finally, she tracked him to earth in the drawing room. Not being especially wealthy, her parents had decorated the townhouse—which had been gifted to her father, along with the country manor, for his service to the Crown when he'd been but a brash young man—quite modestly. There were no gilt frames or chair legs here, but it was pretty and elegant, and the drawing room was one of her favorites. Not as much as Briar Cottage—which is what her mother had named the manor house—but there were worse places in the world to call home, and she was extremely fortunate for this one.

After the scandal in her own life that had ruined her reputation. As if she cared a jot for that. It was all quite silly, really, that the English *ton* put such value on whether a woman was an innocent, or heaven forbid she enjoyed the act of intercourse. Truly, it was no one's business, and didn't make a woman bad.

What would they say if they knew she carried a dagger disguised as a pair of stylish scissors on her person most of the time? Not that she cared. She hadn't been birthed to dance attendance on society matrons whom she'd never met and wouldn't have liked if she had. Life was much too precious for all of that.

"There you are!" Her brother sat on a low sofa, bent over with his elbows resting upon his knees and his hands dangling between his legs, looking for all the world as if he'd been told it would rain for the next hundred years and every field he owned—thanks to their father's will—would flood eternally. "Why have you been hiding? It's quite unlike you."

A yap from Kip reinforced her annoyance.

Conor raised his head, and as Olivia came closer, the desolation in his gray eyes frightened her. "I have had much on my mind and needed time to try and find words to tell you."

Oh, dear. That didn't bode well. "It cannot be all bad. We have come through tough times, but your import business should come back to life soon as everything comes back to normal." Yes, the prior year had nearly devastated them, yet Conor had a good head for business, and he was as resourceful as their father had been. All the time he'd told her he had multiple revenue streams that would see them through until the imports righted themselves.

And anything was better than being forced to struggle merely to survive in Ireland. Even though she and Conor were third-generation Irish, and they had been born in England, their looks and slight lilt in the voice made them instantly less than in some of the higher-born English's eyes.

Not that she cared a fig for that either. She was proud of her heritage and meant to make something of herself, just as her parents had done.

"This has nothing to do with the business." Conor rubbed a hand along the side of his face, then shoved those fingers through his mop of red hair that tended to curl. "However, there is good news, for I did receive a rather large payment which will keep things afloat for many months."

"That sounds promising." Her brother was well-connected and charming enough that he could make deals at the drop of a hat. In that, he was much like their father, whereas she'd inherited her mother's wicked temper, slightly snubbed nose, and an overabundance of freckles.

He scrambled to his feet. "Please, sit. I cannot tell this story with you floating about."

Knots of worry pulled in her belly as Olivia sat on a chair that matched the sofa he'd just vacated. The crushed mauve velvet would always remind her of her sweet mother. "What has occurred to send you into such a pelter?"

Kip pawed at her slippers until she picked him up and settled him into her lap.

With a sigh that sounded as if it had come from his toes, Conor met her gaze. "Two nights ago, I went with a friend to the Lyon's Den gaming hell."

"You already know your penchant for losing at the tables," she said with annoyance in her voice. "Wagering isn't your skill set."

"I am well aware of that, Olivia," he fairly spat out as he took to pacing in front of her chair. "But I was bored and a little desperate waiting for things to right themselves." For the space of a few heartbeats, he was silent. "Eventually, I *did* win a few hands, so I was more confident. When I sat down to faro with a couple of men much more skilled, that was when the trouble started."

"And you were quickly in the weeds," she concluded, for that was how it always went with her brother. He would go gambling, lose much, then stay away from the tables for months on end before he was lured back. Coming to London was the worst thing for him even if it was crucial for his business. "Some of these Town friends are not good influences."

"My circle of contacts is about to grow exponentially, though."

"How is that?" She stroked Kip's soft fur and hoped for the best.

Conor turned and met her gaze once more. "I, uh… Well, the last game I played, I lost and couldn't cover the debt, so I, er, offered your hand in marriage instead."

Utter silence rang in the room directly following his statement.

For long moments, Olivia stared at him as her anger slowly built. Even Kip shook in her lap, from rage or from fear, she couldn't say. "I beg your pardon, but you did what?" she asked in the deceptively low whisper that usually sent the people who knew her scuttling. This would destroy all of her carefully laid plans.

Some of the color faded from her brother's face. He cleared his throat and drew himself up to his tallest height. "I gambled away your hand at the faro table, and now you will be wed."

"How could you, Conor?" Annoyance and disappointment twisted down her spine. Yet it wasn't wholly his fault. All the way back to their grandfather—possibly even before that—her relatives had always been bold, rash, and determined to succeed. Perhaps her brother had fallen victim to that, for she hoped to do the same for herself. "I don't wish to marry right now, and to a man I've not met." Good lord, had he gambled away her future to a horrid lord with a paunch and garlic-scented breath? A man with a passel of children who needed yet another mother?

"Don't come the crab at me, Sis. Since Papa died, you have become my responsibility alone."

"I can look after myself." She resented the fact he thought her incapable.

"Oh, I well know how you do that." Conor shook his head and his gaze turned shrewd. "Besides, this is your best hope for a respectable life after what you did." Her multiple scandals loomed unspoken between them. "Truly, I'm damned fortunate to make this deal." A hint of his Irish lilt came out, a testament to his emotional state. "You will marry into the *beau monde*. Be a lady. Command respect."

Olivia couldn't help but point her gaze to the ceiling. "I have no use for all of that." In her heart of hearts, her dream was to open a clinic that could serve as a safe haven for women who had been wronged or mistreated by lying men. It would be somewhere they could turn to for comfort and support, a place that would help them survive. It certainly would have helped her a time or two.

Either that or create a liaison between orphanages and couples eager to find children when they couldn't have any of their own. Already, she worked with an orphanage in the country not far from their home and delivered knitted blankets to keep the young ones warm. It kept her hands busy while she plotted revenge.

She hadn't quite decided how to give back to society, but it would happen soon. There was a certain feeling in her bones that her grandmother would have said was an inkling into the future. While her roots had provided a plethora of wonderful things, they didn't have reach or privilege, but they certainly had stubbornness.

None of that would help her now, especially with her plans for revenge. "I have no time for an unwanted marriage."

"It can't be helped. The contracts have already been signed and a fat settlement deposited into my account at the bank."

"What?" Curling her fingers too tightly into Kip's fur, she eased off when he yelped and wriggled from her lap. "Why the devil would a man in his right mind give *you* funding before a marriage? Shouldn't you have had a dowry for me to give *him*?"

"I didn't have a say in it. Once I was shuttled up to an office and spoken to by a Mrs. Dove-Lyon, she arranged everything. Made me sign paperwork." Amusement danced in his eyes, which was an odds with the circumstances. "I had the feeling she'd done similar stunts quite a few times. Also, your husband-to-be was quite livid about both my settlement and what he'd been required to give to you."

"That doesn't make me feel better." She *would not* marry this man, regardless of what he had given her brother.

"It matters not." Conor waved a hand in dismissal as if he was already putting on airs. "In two days, you'll marry Lord Ashbury, and that will be that." Then his whole expression crumpled into pleading. "You must do this else I'll be tossed in debtor's prison, or she'll take Papa's business. Those were my choices."

"What?" Shock plowed into her chest and left her a prisoner in her chair as she gawked at him. "Did you say Lord Ashbury?"

"Indeed. How odd is it that he's our closest neighbor in the country, yet you're essentially being forced to wed him thanks to a gaming hell in London?"

"Yes, the irony of it isn't lost to me," she muttered beneath her breath. For long moments, she simply stared at her brother. She went hot and cold by turns. *I'm to wed the viscount.* The dratted man who'd caused her best friend's death, the man on whom she wished revenge. "I don't know what to say."

"Ah, changed your mind now that you know who the groom is to be?" Shrewdness twinkled in his eyes. "Or are you trying to save your only sibling from a horrible fate?"

"The second one, of course." Shock still held much sway with her. She was being handed the object of her displeasure, offered as unwitting sacrifice, put directly into her clutches. "The man doesn't matter, but I am still quite angry at you for making me choose between your freedom or mine."

It wasn't fair, but then, when had life ever been that?

Sadness crept into his expression. "I'm sorry. What would you have me do?"

"Obviously, there is nothing we can do at this point." She glanced at Kip, who sat near her chair and looked back with his tongue hanging out. It was almost a perfect plan, for she could have her revenge with no one the wiser, except she would need to marry Ashbury in two days. Too bad there would be no time to poison the blackheart during an engagement period.

"Well?" He stared pointedly at her.

Olivia frowned. "Well, what?"

He huffed. "Will you marry the viscount, or will I have to strongarm or guilt you into it?"

"As if you haven't done that already?"

Try as she might, she couldn't summon an image of Ashbury into her mind. Over the course of her life, she'd probably only seen him a handful of times in passing. When Cynthia had told her she had a highflyer for a lover, never would she have suspected it had been the viscount. Even in the end when Cynthia lay dying, she hadn't known, and by the time she'd rushed to the cottage where she'd lived with her parents, Cynthia had already passed. The viscount had never made an appearance, at least not while she'd been there.

However, his reputation had preceded him. He indulged in as many vices as London could provide, and from all accounts, he hadn't been back to his country estate in a handful of years. No one knew why, and he didn't offer an explanation.

Dear God! She sucked in a breath. That brief blurb in the paper about his impending nuptials had been about her. *I am being forced to wed Lord Ashbury.*

Could she make the needed sacrifice? Would he remember what he'd done, or even remember Cynthia? And more to the point, did she have the courage to kill him? A life for a life?

Those questions could not be answered just now. A sick feeling rose into her throat as she gripped the arms of her chair. Her brother's stare became overwhelming. Finally, she gave a curt nod. "I suppose I will do it, but not for you."

He frowned. "For whom, then?"

"Me." Slowly, she rose to her feet.

"Due to your ruined reputation?"

"No." Olivia shook her head. "For personal reasons." Conor didn't need to know why. No one did, for that matter. If she couldn't kill the viscount, she could certainly make his life miserable until she decided he'd paid his penance. "At least this way I won't be your responsibility any longer, so you needn't worry, and my future will be secure." If she didn't manage to see the viscount lifeless, she would have more power and influence as his wife than she did currently as a mere member of the gentry. That would put a clinic within reach for whatever avenue she chose to pursue.

"Well, that takes the burden from my shoulders." Her brother came close and laid a hand on her arm. "Thank you. It's much to ask of you, but I'm glad you will have someone in your life besides me." Then he took her hand. "Believe it or not, I've been worried about you for a long time. You've been... distant lately, as if you're wrestling with a problem you haven't shared."

To Olivia's mortification, her chin trembled. It had been quite a while since she'd felt as if she'd had anyone on her side or to confide in. "I, uh, I suppose I have spent too long in my own head. After

Cynthia died, I... lost focus." She refused to go into all that fueled her at the moment, but he did know of the grief she'd struggled with.

"I'm sorry you are still having such a difficult time." Conor squeezed her fingers. "You and Cynthia were thick as thieves for a while, much to Papa's dismay." He gave her a wry look. "He didn't like how you kept company with a maid."

"As if rank or position matters between anyone." She shook her head. "Cynthia was the sweetest friend a girl could ever have, and in the country, class divides seemed less than they do here." Blinking away the traces of moisture in her eyes, Olivia sighed. "We had such plans for our lives." True, marriage had been among those plans, but they had vowed never to be very far away from each other.

Then the dratted viscount put an end to all of that.

"Perhaps it's time for you to find happiness again," he said softly before leaning over and bussing her cheek. "There's no harm in moving past the bad things in order to usher in something better."

She snorted. "Better with Lord Ashbury? I hardly think that is possible."

"He is merely what every other titled lord in London is, but that is not reason to hold his life against him." Conor shrugged. "Their world isn't ours even though it might overlap at times."

"I don't want just another lord for my husband." In fact, she hadn't given a spouse much thought, for if she'd like a man enough to have relations with him, that's what she'd done. Her last affair had ended in scandal and disaster, which had soured her from trusting men again, but that didn't mean the flame of hope still didn't burn bright in her chest. "I always thought the man I'd eventually marry would be... exceptional and different."

"You don't know that Ashbury won't be. He certainly commanded attention and respect at the Lyon's Den. Even if Mrs. Dove-Lyon seemed a bit annoyed at him when we were signing the contracts."

"Ah." What had the viscount to be annoyed about? She was the one giving up her freedom and the whole of her life while his wouldn't change all that much. It didn't matter. Nothing did except taking her revenge on the man. "I will need a gown. Something stunning to mark the occasion. I should probably look my best for my wedding day, don't you think?"

"Yes, but the cost of expediting a gown—"

"Shouldn't be an issue since Ashbury gave you a settlement," she interrupted with narrowed eyes. "Consider it your last gift to me before some other man has the undertaking of my care." Perhaps once she'd made it beyond obvious to the viscount that they wouldn't suit, that she would never come 'round to the fact she was his wife, he might agree to let her live out her life at his country estate. It was where she felt most at home.

"Fine." Conor shook his head. "I truly am sorry I put you in this position."

That didn't quell the anger sitting hot in her chest. "Promise me that from this point onward, you will curb the penchant for gaming. You are hopeless at it, and there is no need to squander your future."

Sadness lingered in his eyes. "It's the least I can do."

"Good." She clicked her tongue. "Come, Kip. We have a trousseau to throw together and trunks to pack." If it was in her power, she would make the viscount sorry he'd ever agreed to this hasty union, and if he thought she would ever love him—let alone give him access to her body—he would soon be shown how wrong he was.

Hopefully, he would regret ever stoking her quick temper.

I'm doing this for you, Cynthia, and I hope you can forgive me for not being there for you in your hour of need.

After all these years, revenge was in sight.

Chapter Three

December 17, 1817
Mrs. Dove-Lyon's private office
The Lyon's Den

Rain hit the windows, and the gray clouds contributed to the gloomy mood as Thomas cooled his heels inside the private office belonging to Mrs. Dove-Lyon. At least she had a fire crackling behind an ornate metal grate, for it was deuced cold, and if that trend continued, the rain would turn to snow.

The perfect setting for love and romance… or a forced marriage. Bah!

Where the devil was the woman? Tired of sitting and knowing she did it on purpose, Thomas launched to his feet in favor of pacing the small space with its comfortable-looking, elegant furniture groupings and the luxurious upholstery and draperies. The lighting was kept low to prohibit clear sight and to no doubt extend the mystery surrounding her.

Finally, a door on one side of the room opened, and the owner of the club came into the room. She didn't alight on a chair as he expected. Instead, she kept to the shadows of the space, much of her form shrouded in the darkness made by the dim lighting.

"Ah, Lord Ashbury. Would you care for tea?" The gentle clink of china echoed in the room as she apparently pulled out a teacup from a tray.

When the deuce had it been delivered and how had he missed it?

"No, thank you." He frowned as he waited on her, once again, while she fixed a cup for herself. Was she always this maddening or was it all an act merely to set him off-guard?

"Why are you here, Ashbury? I thought I'd made everything perfectly clear for you when the contracts were signed."

"Ah, you must mean when you accomplished separating me from my coin." It was bad enough she'd practically demanded that he give Mr. Jameson two thousand pounds for the *honor* of marrying his sister, but then she'd also made certain he'd settled the same amount on the woman's head to be held for her use, no questions asked. To say nothing of promising her pin money which she could use without his consent or agreement.

"It is only fair. Some of you within the *beau monde* have more money than intellect, and since the people you hold beneath your heel are unable to fight back, I must do that for them." Of course Mrs. Dove-Lyon chose a chair that was mostly shrouded in shadow so he couldn't see her all that well, and bizarrely enough, she wore a bonnet with a dark, filmy veil hiding over the top half of her face. Why? To maintain the mystery or was she truly that deep into mourning that it had now become a daily part of her toilette?

Not that he could fault her if that were the case. There was still a gaping hole in his heart from the loss of Cynthia.

He frowned at the not-so-subtle insult, but then, she didn't truly know him. "So I am to pay for the sins of other men?"

"Not at all."

"Then you should disabuse yourself of the notion I need this forced marriage. I am quite happy being on my own, and I cannot imagine the woman involved will appreciate being coerced to the altar."

"So arrogant and so blind," she said in a low voice, then paused to take a sip from her teacup. "There are things in your life you should atone for, Ashbury. Things that only redemption will fix."

What the devil did that mean? "You assume that you should judge me for my life choices as well as carry out an execution, as it were?" How disillusioned could one person be?

"Hardly." Her chuckle reverberated in the air, but it also served as a light warning. "I have never considered myself better or more sterling in values or decisions than anyone else. Perhaps the opposite is more true." After resting her teacup on a small rose-inlaid table at her elbow, she rested her hands in her lap. The pale skin was a stark contrast against the dark skirting. "If you can honestly tell me that everything in your existence is perfect and you are truly happy, I will gladly withdraw the contracts."

Damn and blast.

He rubbed the fingers of one hand over an eye. "It is not, and you know it." Which was why she had him over a barrel. A huff of frustration escaped him. "I haven't been happy—truly or otherwise—in a while." Not since his life was upended and nothing was ever the same. After he lost Cynthia, his mother succumbed to death two years later. Three years after that, his father died from an attack of the heart.

I have known nothing except death for far too long.

For long moments, Mrs. Dove-Lyon remained silent as she stared at him from the shadows. "While I am sorry to hear that, until you can square with your past transgressions, you will continue to suffer. Perhaps over the course of the upcoming holidays, you can find what is missing in your life, and if not, I pray you are able to find peace."

"In the meanwhile, both I and my bride-to-be must suffer, especially if we don't suit." It sounded positively horrid. "Nice little matchmaking scheme you run here." Not even she would be able to ignore the sarcasm and bitterness in his tone. Now he knew what Pennington had struggled with.

"Everyone requires a catalyst at some point, Lord Ashbury. Only you can decide if your marriage will be just that." When he tried to offer a protest, she lifted a hand, palm outward. "This conversation has finished. What you should do now is prepare yourself for your impending nuptials."

"Tomorrow."

"Yes, and should you think to not go through with them, I will make an appearance. If the ceremony doesn't go off, I have my statement ready to go out to any and all interested parties regarding your little... hobby." If there was a threat in her voice, he couldn't detect it, but they both knew there was all the same.

Damn. If that knowledge of his political cartoons got out, if those interested parties knew who it was who'd run their names and reputations through the muck, he would have no recourse except to escape to the country. Perhaps for the remainder of his days. There was every possibility his reputation, his wealth, his power and influence could be destroyed or at the very least revoked depending on the ire of his opponents.

He shoved a hand through his hair. "At least tell me about the woman I'm to take to wife." In less than four and twenty hours.

"She has Irish roots, is eight and twenty, is headstrong, and has had her fair share of scandal."

"Of course." So much bitterness in that response. Irish. Good God. "Who. Is. It?" he asked from around clenched teeth.

"Her name is Olivia Rose Jameson, and truth be told, your union won't be dull."

"No doubt you are quite right." Thomas shook his head. "If you won't cooperate, then I shall take my leave."

"Remember, Ashbury, the more troublesome the woman, the greater the chance she will have an impact on your life you won't soon forget." Amusement wove through her words, but he couldn't see her face properly due to the veils and shadows. "Every man says he wants a docile woman who is meek and mild, when the opposite is true in every way."

A grunt was his only response, but he headed across the room for the door. The woman was entirely too impossible.

Remarkably, she chuckled. "Christmastide will never be the same! Mark my words!" she called after him.

Thomas slammed the door to prevent a bitter reply. There was nothing else to do but go home. Any chance of having a love like his parents' was gone, for it would be hopeless with a stranger. Even if he had wanted to marry.

Which he did not. Being forced into it was akin to torture.

Damn them all.

December 17, 1817
Ashbury House
Manchester Square
London, England

THOMAS' NERVES FELT strung too tight. He paced the space in front of the drawing room windows, for it was nearly noon and soon the nuptial ceremony would take place. Though it was insufferable he was being forced into a marriage—Mrs. Dove-Lyon could have relented if she'd truly wished, but instead, she apparently wanted him to suffer—there wasn't another option. Mr. Jameson didn't really deserve to be tossed into a debtor's prison and Thomas would fight to keep his name anonymous with regards to his political drawings.

He had to believe they did a bit of good and directed the people's attention to corruption and wrongs within the government and aristocracy.

Yet he was being forced to make the sacrifice.

Pausing at one of the windows, he blew out a breath as he peered down at the streets within his Manchester Square neighborhood. He adored the area for its quiet charm and the green space contained within the backside of all the buildings. Removed from the larger and more affluent sections of Mayfair, he could almost find peace here if he would let himself. Though he had held the dream in his heart of making Cynthia the townhouse's mistress, he couldn't bear to sell the property or move because the locale was second to none.

To say nothing of the fact he had fond memories of his parents while they were here, and if he were fanciful, he could still feel the force of their love.

Obviously, I have been reading far too much poetry for my own good. For he didn't believe in true love. Not anymore. Not after losing Cynthia. Raising a hand, he traced a gloved fingertip over the plain silver band hidden beneath his fine lawn shirt. He kept it with him always, hanging on a thin bit of leather. It had been meant for her as a wedding band, but now he wore it every day as a talisman of sorts, a reminder to keep grief close, like armor almost, to safeguard his heart.

Not that he had any intentions of losing it.

The rustle of fabric and low buzz of voices filtered into his thoughts, and he turned to see his meager collection of guests coming into the room. He nodded to Pennington as well as the man's countess—both looking quite dapper this morning—and he gave a tight grin to Captain Huxley as he came in behind them. Mr. Jameson brought up the rear of the odd procession, and when his gaze met Thomas', relief crossed the other man's features.

Had he assumed Thomas wouldn't have shown?

Annoyance cut through his chest, for he was bloody tired of people assuming things about him that simply weren't true. When Simon broke away from the group and joined him, Thomas offered a nod. "Thank you for coming."

"I wouldn't have missed this." He winked. "I'm curious to see if you will actually go through with it."

"There is no other choice," he said with much bitterness riding on those words. "The damned contracts are already drawn up, the vicar secured. Mrs. Dove-Lyon wouldn't be talked out of the deal."

"What does she take out from the arrangement?"

He shrugged. "Coin? The knowledge she has destroyed my life?" Briefly, he told his friend about the settlements he'd been made to give both the Jamesons. "I may be forced to wed the woman, but she will never have my heart. That was lost ages ago."

"I'm sorry for whatever you struggle with that you haven't trusted me—or even Pennington—with, but it is my sincere hope you can work through it and perhaps heal from it with this marriage." Nothing except truth reflected in the man's eye. "You deserve peace, Ashbury. We all do."

"Thank you." Those words sent a wad of emotion into his throat. Quickly, he swallowed it down. "I will keep you updated."

The captain clapped a hand to Thomas' shoulder. "Best of luck, my friend. I will remember you when I'm getting my rocks off with the beautiful members of the demimonde and you have been wed to a cold fish."

"Do shut up." But Simon wasn't wrong. Hell, he didn't know what his wife-to-be looked like other than what Mrs. Dove-Lyon had told him.

When Simon went to sit next to Lady Pennington—no doubt hoping to charm her—the earl approached Thomas next.

"I don't have much advice for you, and neither will I try to offer comforting words, for I stood where you are now not long ago." Stark honesty and compassion shone in the earl's eyes. "However…"

"Ugh." Thomas rolled his eyes. "I'm to buck up and soldier on?"

"Perhaps." He offered a grin. "The longer you resist, the more difficult it will be. Now that I have been through the gauntlet, perhaps this is the best thing for you."

"Ha." Thomas shook his head. "I want to be left alone."

"We all assume that, but I have seen the shadows in your eyes and know you have secret pain you haven't shared with me." The earl laid a hand on his shoulder. "Perhaps in this you can find forgiveness in her—with her—so you can finally reach a place of contentment."

"That is a tall order." He couldn't imagine ever being close enough to a stranger to share his history or any sort of intimacy.

"I once thought the same, but keep an open mind, Thomas. I speak from experience. You might come to love your wife. I did, after a while and a bit of a struggle."

"That is an entirely different scenario." Thomas blew out a breath. "You and your wife are well-matched. Mine comes from the gentry and has nothing to recommend her and she's Irish besides."

Not that such ancestry was the worst thing a person could be.

"None of that matters when the blinders come off the eyes and the walls around hearts fall." He offered an encouraging grin. "Think about what I've said. I am always available if you should need to talk."

"I appreciate that." Thomas nodded as Pennington went to join his wife and Simon on one of the low sofas.

Then Wallace, the butler, was at the open double-doors. He nodded to Thomas and stood back in order to usher the woman who would soon be his viscountess into the room.

Damn and blast.

He hadn't expected her to be so striking. Perhaps a few inches over five feet, she moved with all the grace and elegance of a duchess, but it was the gown of dark green satin that set off her pale skin and had her clear gray eyes popping. Red hair collected in the back of her head in an abundance of curls, long strands of which barely brushed her shoulders. Gold embroidery decorated the hem of the gown as well as the rounded bodice that showed the tops of her breasts and unexpectedly fired his imagination. The woman had been born for sinning, of that there was no doubt, but when her gaze crashed into his, the intensity of the hate and fury warring for dominance in those gray pools surprised him.

What was that reaction for? They didn't know each other, and if it was for the nuptial ceremony, it was hardly *his* fault.

There was no time to react, for a lanky man with thinning white hair came into the drawing room next followed by a much younger man who would no doubt serve as a clerk. Both approached Thomas' position.

The older man offered a smile. "You are Lord Ashbury?"

Who the hell else would I be... in my own home? "Yes."

"Lovely. I am Mr. Adamson, the vicar who will conduct your nuptial ceremony." The clergyman gestured with his chin to the young man who'd come in with him. "That is my clerk, Mr. Rodgers. The register will be handled by him, as will any questions you might have following the ceremony." He took a well-loved copy of the *Book of Common Prayer* from the younger man while glancing at Miss Jameson. "Good morning."

"Good morning to you." The veriest hint of an Irish accent drifted through those dulcet tones. Well, that was a relief. At least his soon-to-be wife didn't sound like a rusty gate. She frowned at the vicar. Nothing in her expression gave away her feelings. Was the animosity in her eyes directed at him—Thomas—or the situation in general? Finally, she sought out her brother. A speaking glance was exchanged between them, and then he focused his attention quickly to the window.

Ah. She *was* furious, but at her brother. And well she should be. Mr. Jameson's lack of skill at the gaming tables had landed them both here. But she was also doing this... *for* him. Why? Very odd indeed.

The vicar cleared his throat. "If there are no more guests coming, shall we begin?"

Thomas blew out a breath. "No time to enjoy these last seconds of freedom, eh, Vicar?" When he glanced over his shoulder, he caught sight of Mrs. Dove-Lyon as she slipped into a chair toward the rear of the room away from the windows. Once more, she wore a bonnet with veils that covered the upper portion of her face. Her charcoal-gray gown and matching pelisse didn't give away any clues as to what her figure might look like. "Damn it all to hell, the devil's own consort has arrived," he muttered beneath his breath.

At his side, Miss Jameson stifled a snort. Was she amused or simply agitated? Too difficult to tell.

With a faint smile, Mr. Adamson led them toward the fireplace, where cheerful flames danced behind a decorative iron grate. "The nuptial couple is ready to begin, so I shouldn't keep them waiting. This *is* a special day, after all."

Thomas thought he might choke on his own ire, but he beat it down admirably. From where he stood and at his height, he towered over his bride-to-be, which wasn't so bad, for he was afforded a peek at her décolletage. Decent breasts. Might take the sting out of a lifetime of incarceration, but that remained to be seen.

"Lord Ashbury, Miss Jameson, please face me." When they did, he opened his book to the appropriate page. "Dearly beloved, we are gathered together here in the sight of God, and in the face of these witnesses, to join together this Man and this Woman in holy Matrimony; which is an honorable estate, instituted of God in the time of man's innocency, signifying unto us the mystical union that is betwixt Christ and his Church…"

Thomas shifted his weight from foot to foot. His concentration was nearly gone, made impossible by the pulse pounding in his ears. In minutes he would say vows to this woman—this stranger—whose hand he'd won at a card table, this woman whom he didn't want, as a wife or otherwise. Whenever he'd dreamed of being a husband, it was to Cynthia, the first woman who'd held his heart, regardless of the differences in class between them. Those hopes had been dashed, and now this was his reality.

A frantic cry rose in his throat, and he quickly tamped it down. This wasn't the life he'd envisioned for himself; this wasn't the way he wished to marry or the woman with whom to pledge his life. *Dearest Cynthia, why did you have to leave so soon?*

His bride-to-be must have heard or suspected his distress, for she turned her head. Mixed in with the annoyance and hatred was compassion, and it was so unexpected, Thomas stared at her a second too long. What was she thinking? For that matter, what would she do when she discovered the man she was marrying had firmly given his heart to a dead woman?

Oblivious to Thomas' mental distress, the vicar continued, his voice an unfortunate monotone as he waxed poetic regarding the holy state of marriage. The urge to dart across the room and pour a double measure of brandy took hold, but Thomas quelled that as well. Drinking during a nuptial ceremony certainly wasn't proper.

This is untenable! It felt all too wrong to give his life—share that life—with a stranger.

Mr. Adamson held his prayer book in his hands, the black leather spine cracked and worn, while he addressed Thomas. "Wilt thou have this Woman to thy wedded Wife, to live together after God's ordinance in the holy estate of Matrimony?" His lips curved with a smile. The poor sot assumed this was a wanted union. "Wilt thou love her, comfort her, honor her, and keep her in sickness and in health; and, forsaking all others, keep thee only unto her, so long as ye both shall live?"

Oh, God. There was no chance to escape now.

Anger formed a knot in his throat. *I can never love this woman.* It had hurt too much the last time, so how could he offer up that organ again? "I..." Could he say the words knowing that he didn't mean them? With a quick glance over his shoulder, his gaze landed on Mrs.

Dove-Lyon. Was it his imagination or did she lean forward in her chair with her lips curved in predatory anticipation? Never would he forgive her. "I will," he uttered from around the wad of emotion stuck in his throat.

"Excellent," Mr. Adamson said. He put a forefinger to the words on one page as he addressed Miss Jameson. "Wilt thou have this Man to thy wedded Husband, to live together after God's ordinance in the holy estate of Matrimony? Wilt thou obey him, and serve him, love him, honor him, and keep him in sickness and in health; and, forsaking all others, keep thee only unto him, so long as ye both shall live?"

Silence brewed in the room while Thomas—and everyone else—waited on her answer. "I, uh…" She touched a gloved fingertip of her right hand to her hip before curling it into her skirting. In voice little more than a whisper, she said, "I will, though it's anyone's guess if I shall *obey* this man. He certainly doesn't command my respect."

A few gasps circled through the guests.

"What?" Thomas gawked at her as shock roiled through his chest. Why the devil did she loathe him that much? They'd never met. At least he didn't recall if they had.

"I won't apologize for my words or feelings," she whispered, and that slight Irish lilt sent shivers of need down his spine.

Surely, he didn't desire this spitfire. She was nothing like the women he tended to favor.

"Do remember this *is* a holy ceremony and shouldn't be taken lightly or in jest," Mr. Adamson said as confusion shadowed his face. He then instructed Thomas to take her right hand in his right, which he then did, and Miss Jameson's hand trembled. Was she nervous or enraged? "Lord Ashbury, please repeat after me…"

Why am I allowing this to happen? Perhaps it was easier than fighting. With solicitous attention, he memorized the handful of words through the anger that built in his chest. "I, Thomas Charles Prestwick, Viscount of Ashbury, take thee Miss Olivia Rose Jameson as my wedded Wife, to have and to hold from this day forward, for better for worse, for richer for poorer, in sickness and in health, to love and to cherish, until death us do part..." His throat tightened as he spoke those most sacred of words that would forever bind him with her, the words he had wanted to say to Cynthia until fate took her from him. He cleared his throat. "... according to God's holy ordinance; and thereto I plight thee my troth."

"It has been a long time since I have seen such emotion from a groom." Obviously, Mr. Adamson assumed he was too much in love with his bride to get through to the end.

"Please release hands. Lord Ashbury, take her left in yours."

His bride paused with her hand held at chest level. For one instant, he thought she might slap him.

"Your hand, Miss Jameson," Thomas demanded in a whisper, and finally she gave it over with a soft huff.

Once they'd done as instructed, Mr. Adamson trained his attention on the woman at Thomas' side. "Miss Jameson, repeat after me." He gave her the words, much like the ones he'd said to Thomas moments before.

The pulse in her neck fluttered, which only served to call his attention to her bosom that was liberally sprinkled with the same golden freckles that lay splashed across her face. "I, Miss Olivia Rose Jameson take thee Thomas Charles Prestwick, Viscount of Ashbury, as my wedded Husband." Her voice broke on the last word. "Even if it is under duress, for I certainly would never have chosen *you* willingly."

"I am so sorry, Olivia," Mr. Jameson said in disruption, but his outburst was quickly subdued by Simon. Perhaps he regretted what he had done at the gaming table or for greedily accepting the settlement Thomas was made to offer. Not that it mattered now.

"Please continue, Miss Jameson," the vicar urged.

With a sigh, she focused on the clergyman instead of her almost husband. "To have and to hold from this day forward, for better for worse, for richer, for poorer, in sickness and in health, to love, cherish, and to obey, until death us do part, according to God's holy ordinance." A sound that was much like a choked sob came from her and she finally sought out his gaze. "And thereto I give thee my troth."

"So many emotions flowing this morning." Mr. Adamson grinned as if he expected betrothal bliss all along. "Please release your hands." To Thomas, he whispered, "Now is the time to offer up a ring and any respects you might have for my services."

"Of course, for why shouldn't I continue to give away all that I own?" Bitterness dripped from his voice. He dug a ring from the pocket of his waistcoat, which he gave to the vicar, who rested it upon his open *Book of Common Prayer* while Thomas then followed it with a small leather pouch as payment and gratuity for services rendered. Why it had to be conducted during the ceremony, he would never know. The oval-shaped emerald surrounded by tiny diamonds sparkled like mad in the anemic December light coming in from the windows as well as the candlelight. The bauble was part of the Ashbury estate jewels and had been given to his mother on the day of her wedding to his father. Eventually his bride would have the rest of the parure, but today was not that day. She would need to do something memorable to secure the jewels.

"Much appreciated." Mr. Adamson murmured a few words, no doubt as a blessing, before returning the ring to him while Miss Jameson removed the glove from her left hand. "You may present the ring to the lady." As soon as Thomas slipped it onto the fourth finger of Miss Jameson's hand, the vicar spoke again, the words directed to him. "Please repeat after me."

Dread mixed with a touch of fear down his spine. This was far too permanent. Would he eventually come to rely on this woman, develop a friendship with her only to open himself up to a wealth of new hurt? Only time would tell. "With this Ring I thee wed, with my Body I thee worship, and with all my worldly Goods I thee endow. In the Name of the Father, and of the Son, and of the Holy Ghost. Amen." He couldn't think of his expectations or responsibilities just yet. It was too soon, for everything.

In the silence following, a tiny huff escaped his new wife. "You will absolutely have *no* access to my body," she warned with nothing but loathing in her gray eyes. "I didn't want this union, yet in order to save my hapless brother, I was given no choice, regardless of my own plans and dreams." In a few tugs, she'd donned her glove.

"We have that in common. I didn't want you either, *Lady* Ashbury," he said in a whispered hiss with emphasis on her new title.

Mr. Adamson frowned as he bounced his gaze between them. "Please kneel while we all pray together."

Thomas kneeled, and when her arm brushed his sleeve as she did the same beside him, anger surged anew at the jolt of awareness that went through him from that accidental touch. As the words of the prayer echoed in the room, he peered at his new bride. Her head was cast downward, but annoyance fairly seethed from her in waves. Then the prayer was over, and he stood. So did his bride.

Mr. Adamson closed his book. "I now pronounce thee husband and wife."

Scattered applause broke out among the gathered guests. He couldn't bear to look at his friends yet or see the speculation in their eyes. *I never wanted this, and now we are both stuck.*

"If you'll please see my clerk to sign the register, then everything will be official," The vicar said with a slight grin.

Thomas glanced at his wife. "After you." When he would have put a hand to the small of her back, she darted out of range.

Then she turned on him like a rabid dog. "Don't think to play the courtly hero with me, Ashbury," she hissed while the vicar moved to greet the few guests. Meanwhile, his wife drilled a finger into his chest. "This marriage is in name only, and I will barely tolerate it. You can live your life while I live mine. Do you understand?"

That merely stoked his own ire. "It doesn't matter how this union came about, we have certain responsibilities to each other as well as the title. That comes first." Except he couldn't see himself bedding her long enough to get her with child just now.

"Fine, but first we'll see if you are strong enough to survive."

He frowned. "Survive what?" But she'd already walked away, for Lady Pennington had hailed her. Damn her eyes, anyway. He'd married a damned harpy, a woman who probably despised bed sport despite the rumors of her reputation. When movement from the corner of his eye caught his attention, he realized Mrs. Dove-Lyon intended to leave the room. With a soft curse, he caught her at the door. "Why have you done this to me when there is nothing except animosity between me and my wife? Possibly hatred on hers, but I've no idea why."

The woman's lips curved into a grin. "If you want answers, Ashbury, you must be willing to look past the end of your nose and climb out of your misery."

"What the devil does that mean?" Why did she always speak in riddles?

"The stubborn and fearful are always the ones who will fall the hardest." Mrs. Dove-Lyon sighed. "Listen closely. You and Pennington have gained far too much coin from my gaming hell, and now you're leading Captain Huxley down that same path. I am not best pleased. Besides, I do have experience in matters of the heart and adore when men must squirm on my hook." She reached up and patted his cheek. "Never forget, Ashbury, that I will always hold the winning hand."

As he stood there like a nodcock searching for a reply, she left the room. The subtle scent of lilacs wafted to his nose, and he turned about to find his bride a few feet away. "It seems we will spend Christmastide in joint misery," he said to her with bitterness dripping from the words.

"Well, you will at least. I intend to fully enjoy myself at your expense." She drew her gaze slowly up and down his person as if she were assessing him, and damn if it didn't send awareness prickling over his skin. "Don't linger at the wedding breakfast, Ashbury. I'm certain we have much to talk about." Then she crossed the room and returned to the countess' side.

More annoyed than he cared to admit, he met Simon's eye, gestured to the corridor with his chin, and then quit the room. His new bride could damn well wait an eternity, for he was not in the habit of taking orders.

Especially from a woman he didn't want and would never love.

CHAPTER FOUR

OLIVIA COULDN'T IGNORE the anger and rage swirling through her belly. She had been wed all of five minutes before her new husband left the room with one of his friends. No doubt they would go drinking in an effort to forget the events of the morning, which meant he would return home well in his cups. Would that he remembered this was a union in name only.

And even if he didn't, she'd make certain he felt the blade of her dagger before they went any further in the relationship.

Then she frowned. *Home.* It now meant that she would be here, in his townhouse as his wife, for the remainder of her days. As she stood watching the Earl of Pennington talk quietly with his wife, her belongings, along with her dog, were being sent over and there would be no need to go back to her brother's house. Would Conor allow her to take refuge there if the need arose? Or would she need to retreat to Ashbury's country estate?

Eventually, the countess broke away and came toward her while the earl stayed back to speak with the vicar and clerk. In her gown of wine silk with her blonde hair caught in a loose chignon at her nape, she was the vision of perfection. "You don't exactly have the look of a bride flushed with happiness."

"That's because I'm not." Olivia couldn't help but snort her derision. "I don't consider the viscount a prize to be won, and neither would I have ever chosen him." At the last second, she gasped and stared at the other woman. "I shouldn't have said that."

"The truth, no matter how unflattering, is always refreshing to hear." The countess smiled and laid a hand on Olivia's arm. "Don't discount the viscount yet. You might not get along with him. You might even loathe him. You might even think this union is merely some colossal joke that fate has played on you, but give things time to settle."

Her first instinct was to protest, but it probably wouldn't have done any good. "Somehow, you sound as if you know what I'm facing."

"Oh, my dear Olivia." The countess uttered a tinkling laugh that was full of amusement. She glanced at her husband, and when he looked over and their gazes connected, an expression of such love came over the other woman's face that jealousy stabbed through Olivia's chest. When she transferred her attention back to Olivia, she gave a wry grin. "I apologize. Marriage is still quite new, and my feelings for Pennington grow with each passing day."

"You are certainly fortunate." Even though she had enjoyed a few lovers in her history, none of them had managed to steal her heart, and she hadn't wanted to wait until love had come along before she experienced what coupling with a man felt like. "I have not stumbled upon love or even romance thus far."

"There is no better way to explore those possibilities than in your marriage." The countess shrugged. "You have no choice but to work together with him, but none of that will happen if you both remain stubborn and continue to hide behind the walls you've built about yourselves."

Olivia sighed. "I don't know if that will be possible. I have very definite and legitimate reasons for hating him."

"I thought I had that too with Pennington." She took Olivia's hand and held her gaze. "The last thing I wanted to do was work with him; I didn't want to understand what drove him, why he was the way he was or have him share the secrets he was keeping."

Despite herself, Olivia was interested in the story. "Did he?"

"Yes, eventually." Her smile held a dreamy edge. "So did I. We both had to give pieces of ourselves and put away our pride in order to find common ground."

Another pang went through Oliva's chest. Would the same ever be possible between her and Ashbury? At the present time, she rather doubted it. "He doesn't know who I am, but I know of him, and it's a convoluted tale wherein I don't think I could ever forgive him." To say nothing of the fact that she wanted to carve out his heart for what he'd done to Cynthia.

"Give it time." The countess squeezed her hand. "But you need to be willing to put in the work. So does he." A faint blush crept across her cheeks. "Oh, and one more thing."

"Yes?"

"Don't discount the power of a kiss."

"But I don't—"

"I know." The countess nodded. She widened her eyes. "Believe me, I *know*. The start of my marriage with Pennington was quite fraught with bullishness and strife and plain dislike, but there is something about kissing a man, of letting yourself be temporarily vulnerable enough to have him so close that can open doors—and hearts—you never thought possible."

For long moments, Olivia shared a look with the other woman before she nodded. "I promise to keep your advice in mind." It would be an uphill battle. For so long she'd let the need for revenge fuel her that she didn't know what else to do.

"That's all I ask." The countess tugged on her hand. "Come. Let me introduce you to my husband." Before Olivia could offer a protest, she was pulled across the room and presented to the earl.

"Pennington, this is the new Lady Ashbury." The countess was so obviously enamored of the man it was almost embarrassing.

"A pleasure to make your acquaintance." The welcoming grin slowly faded from his face as he stared at her. "Though your union was forced and manipulated by the owner of the Lyon's Den, please don't hurt my best friend." Though he was welcoming enough, there was a low-banked anger in the backs of his eyes that made her wary. "Thomas has been through things he hasn't even told me about, things that put great sadness in his expression. He keeps himself aloof from feeling anything, but it's my sincere hope you might be able to help him."

"With what?" Truly, she was confused. She had gone into this marriage with nothing except loathing in her heart for the viscount. Now, when both the earl and the countess had more or less stood in the gap for his character, some of her previous confidence had been shaken. "I know nothing about him outside of the fact that he killed my best friend."

Pennington's eyebrows rose in surprise. He exchanged a glance with his wife. "I find that difficult to believe. Ashbury is the friend everyone wishes they had. He is kind and compassionate when he wants to be, and fiercely loyal when he has reason."

"Ha! That is *not* the impression of the man I have at all." She touched her fingertips to the dagger hidden beneath her skirting. It rested in a leather sheath strapped to her right thigh, and she couldn't wait to employ it. "He needs to pay for what he did, for what he destroyed."

Again, he rested his gaze on her. Speculation and confusion warred for dominance in his expression. "If that is so, he has kept such news close to his chest, and that is perhaps what he struggles with the most. This marriage might break him." The earl paused as he glanced at his wife. "Or it might be exactly what he needs. Help him heal, Miss Jameson—Lady Ashbury. Every year that goes by, my friend slips farther away from me and into the past. I… I want him back."

Such an impassioned plea sent uncertainty skittering through her gut. Had she made a wrong assessment about the viscount? "I cannot make any promises, Your Lordship." Olivia refused to waver from her own plans merely because the earl cared about his friend. "There is far too much at stake, too much hurt to just forget due to marriage."

"But you need to—"

The countess laid a hand on his arm as Pennington's voice raised. "This is not our concern. Much like what happened to us—between us—Ashbury and his wife will need to find their own footing." She offered a small smile to Olivia. "If you should have need of either of us, though, please don't hesitate to call or send a messenger."

"Thank you." As she nodded, the couple drifted out of the room, no doubt to partake of the wedding breakfast. Perhaps that was where the vicar and his clerk had gone, for they were no longer in the room.

And she was left alone with her brother.

Conor didn't waste time in closing the distance between them. "Truly, I'm sorry you are trapped in a marriage you didn't want," he began in a voice choked with emotion. "If I could do things over again—"

"Do hush. You are making it worse than it is." Heat slapped at her cheeks. "I will suffer through to the bitter end if need be, but this is the last favor I will do for you." She met his gaze and didn't give quarter. "Curb your ways, Conor. No more wagering or spending your coin on vices that don't matter. I suspect I'll lose my new husband to such things; I don't want to lose my brother as well."

"Of course." He nodded as if he were a marionette on a string. "I promise." Then he sobered and took her hand. "Will you please come home for Christmas dinner? It won't be the same without you."

"Now you have *my* promise." Christmastide was one of her favorite times of the year. When their parents had been alive, she'd helped her mother decorate the house, plan all the baked goods, and then distribute them to the servants and tenants. "I cannot let you eat alone, regardless of whether Ashbury already has plans." And well he might if he and Pennington were that close, but she owed her new husband nothing except a stab wound that may or may not bleed out.

"You have my apologies for making your life more difficult." He squeezed her fingers.

Olivia appreciated the support. "Perhaps this will afford a change I so desperately need." After talking with the countess, she suspected she couldn't keep living only for revenge. It was destroying her from the inside out.

"Such as?"

"Prison?" She shrugged and chuckled at his look of concern. A sigh left her throat. "I don't know. Perhaps this marriage will make me feel something besides grief and anger. I grow weary of losing the people in my life I love, even if that is the way of things."

Her brother nodded. "Let us go into breakfast. I would like to offer my congratulations to your husband."

"If he is even in attendance." There was no way of knowing where the bounder had gone to when he'd left the room with his friend.

It would be a long day, no doubt.

That night

THOUGH OLIVIA'S NERVES were jumpy, and she didn't know what to expect, she had to admit that Ashbury House in the Manchester Square neighborhood was quite lovely. In the spring and summer when the foliage and flowers were at their height, the gardens of the square at the rear of the buildings would be gorgeous. She couldn't wait to explore them.

Now, she was in the suite of rooms the viscount had given her. Whatever else he was—or was not depending on what the truth was—his house was run with quiet precision. Whoever had decorated these rooms had certainly had the talent for it. Golds, pinks, and the veriest hints of light blues went through the draperies, rugs, counterpane, as well as the delicately striped paper that covered some of the walls. The other walls had been painted with that faint blue, and while the tone was quite feminine, there was also a certain calm present here that she appreciated. The windows overlooked the rear gardens and the square beyond.

No doubt Kip would enjoy many hours of walking through the area and scaring rabbits and the like.

She threw a glance to the pallet in one corner of the bedchamber she'd made for the Pomeranian. Apparently, enduring a move to a different house had exhausted the poor canine, for he was a ball of russet fur and not inclined to wake.

As she passed into the adjoining dressing and sitting room, Olivia appreciated the soft illumination from a few candles. A shiver went down her spine, whether from apprehension or the ambient chill, she couldn't say, but she drew her hands up and down her arms to stimulate warmth. What would happen tonight, her wedding night? Though she had warned her husband during the nuptial ceremony this union would be in name only, it remained to be seen if he would abide by those wishes.

Not that he probably cared. Though he'd attended the wedding breakfast, the bastard had acted as if she didn't exist as he ate and talked and laughed with his friends, leaving her to stew and hate him more while she'd sat in silence with Conor. Following breakfast, the viscount had removed from the townhouse with his captain friend in tow. As of an hour ago, he hadn't deigned to return, so she'd been much on her own for the bulk of the day and evening. Not that she'd minded, for she'd taken that opportunity to explore the house and introduce herself to the servants, who had all eyed her with an odd mixture of open interest and hope.

Why? What had they'd already been through with the viscount she hadn't been privy to?

With a tight grin, Olivia removed the sheath and her dagger—a slim knife, really—that doubled as a pair of ivory-handled scissors from her thigh. The blades she kept sharp in the event she would ever come upon Lord Ashbury, and now her chance was nigh. The pair of scissors were given to her by her father on the occasion of her sixteenth birthday, for he was a big proponent of women being able to defend themselves.

There was a whole history of wrongs committed against the Irish to lend credence to his claim, so she hadn't questioned it. Besides, it was a functional gift, for she adored knitting.

The soft *snick* of the door opening wrenched her from her thoughts. She smiled in welcome and gratitude at her maid, Bess. In some relief, she wilted into a delicate chair with a brocade cushion. "I'm glad it's you instead of *him*."

Bess gasped at the sight of the blade. "Good evening, miss. Or should I say, my lady."

That dratted title again. "Don't mind me." Heat infused her cheeks as she laid the scissors on a small table nearby. "I was merely woolgathering."

"Do you require assistance with undressing?"

"Most likely." The gown was quite extravagant and a departure from what she usually wore, but she'd wanted to make an impression and match her newly elevated status. Seeing Bess gave her a sense of normalcy, and she supposed she should be thankful the viscount let her bring the maid. "Though I am not here for romance." Or even a quick toss in the sheets, no matter that her new husband was handsome enough. There was something about his blond hair that curled just so at his collar or the way his light brown eyes had the appearance of tea in the light.

But revenge took precedence.

"Very well. Let me get out the night clothes you requested."

Ah yes, the outfit she'd shopped for that would hopefully guarantee the viscount's interest and distract him enough so she could put her blade into his heart. "Thank you." She frowned as Bess laid the silky, lace-edged night dress and thin matching robe over the back of a chair. "It was fortunate the owner of my favorite shop could make the garment in two days."

"No doubt it helped that you already had the fabric."

"True." Thanks to her brother's importing business. The hue of light blue went with the theme of the suite even if she'd not known of the color scheme.

It took next to no time to exchange the green gown and underclothes for the night set. Olivia moved to the other room and refreshed herself behind the privacy screen with birds and flowers painted on the silk. When she came out, Bess was turning down the bed.

"Would you like a tray of food sent up? Surely, you must be hungry since you didn't come down for dinner." There was no judgment in her voice, only curiosity.

The thought of food just now when she was by turns anxious and angry nearly turned her stomach. "If I am peckish, I'll ring for you." Restless, she stepped in front of the cheval glass and admired the frothy creation and how it laid on her body. The silk was deliciously cool against her skin.

"If you are sure?"

"I am, but thank you."

"Goodnight, my lady. I hope tonight is everything you have dreamed about with a husband." Quietly, Bess left through the corridor door and closed it tight behind her.

Olivia frowned. She glanced at Kip, who snored away in his pallet, then she moved to the window and once more peered out, but the darkness prevented her from seeing much of anything except her own reflection. What type of man was the viscount, truly? All she'd thought she knew of him conflicted with what Pennington and his wife had hinted at. Who was right?

Not that her own past had been sterling. Yes, she had taken a few lovers, and once there had been the expectation of a tiny dream that hadn't come to fruition. She'd flown in the highest highs and despaired in the lowest lows. If things were different and she'd met Ashbury through proper society channels, there was every reason he wouldn't want her anyway, for she wasn't as pristine or simpering as a bride should be, according to the *ton's* matrons.

She blew out a frustrated breath and turned away from the window. It was better to concentrate on her ever-simmering anger, for it kept grief and disappointment at bay, as well as thoughts that would dwell on both.

Before she could decide whether to slip into bed with a book or go down and sneak some edibles from the kitchen, the corridor door once more opened, but this time, the viscount came into the room looking a bit rough and ragged around the edges. Somehow, he'd lost his tailcoat. His cravat was loose, his hair ruffled, and the dark shadow of stubble clung to his cheeks and chin, rendering him far too handsome for his own good.

The first thing his gaze fell upon was Kip. "What the hell is that?"

"A dog. *My* dog." Olivia rolled her eyes as her heartbeat tripped wildly through her veins. This was much different than seeing him during the ceremony, for she was well and truly alone, and his powerful presence filled the space. "His full name is Sir Kippington-Prestwick, but I call him Kip." Then she gave him a saccharine-sweet smile. "After you. I felt you should be remembered in this way."

"That is not a dog, madam. It is but an oversized rat." He narrowed his eyes as the dog barked with exception to the slight. "Why does it bear my name?"

"After you killed my best friend—"

"I have no idea to what you refer," he interrupted with a warning in his baritone.

"So you say. Regardless, I had a difficult time coming to terms with her loss." An unexpected wad of emotion lodged in her throat. "Her parents gave me Kip as a puppy so I wouldn't feel alone," she finished in a whisper.

"But why name him after me?" He darted a glance between her and the dog.

"To never forget what you did, to make me always remember you needed a comeuppance." Could he not sense her ire?

"Lovely." Sarcasm fairly dripped from the word. "Put that sorry excuse for a dog in the dressing room. I would rather not bed you with an audience." In his cups, but not so deep he had difficulties functioning, he cut quite a commanding and slightly dangerous figure.

I would rather not bed you at all. But to head off an argument that might thwart her plans, Olivia crossed the room, scooped Kip into her arms, and carried him into the other room. With instructions for him to behave, she returned to the adjoining bedchamber—grabbing the knife on her way out, and softly closed the door behind her. Quickly, she hid the blade within the voluminous folds of her skirting. "Do not think to order me about as if I am nothing."

"Do not think to antagonize me so early in our union."

She snorted. "Ah, because you coming into my private rooms demanding I bed you while you reek of brandy is the utmost in charming?"

"You are my wife." He glared at her.

Not giving quarter, Olivia glared back. "In name only, remember, so that does not entitle you to anything I am not willing to give." It wouldn't be long now. She renewed her grip on the blade's handle. So close to having her revenge.

"Eventually, I will need an heir." The viscount crossed his arms at his chest, which only served to call her attention to the sweep of his shoulders and the solidness of his torso. What would it feel like to find herself pressed against him?

"That night is not this one." Despite her thirst for revenge, she took a few steps backward as he suddenly advanced on her.

"Bah! What have I need for a troublesome woman anyway?"

"Yet it is all too proper for me to be trapped with a man of your ilk? Quite the double standard, wouldn't you say?"

He threw up a hand. "You are impossible!"

"And you are repugnant!" Tension fairly snapped and crackled between them.

"I never wanted this damned marriage."

"Neither did I."

"Yet your bloody brother must have charmed Mrs. Dove-Lyon or at least pleaded his case to her better than I did mine, for here we are, and I was made to pay for the damned privilege as well." Anger and annoyance growled through his voice, yet it stoked the awareness she had of him already dancing over her skin.

The last thing she wanted was to bond with him over a mutual dislike of being forced to wed, but he needed to understand that what he did to Cynthia went beyond the pale, whether he wanted to admit it or not. "Then we need to come to an understanding of sorts before our respective anger destroys... everything."

His eyes narrowed further. "Meaning?"

"Meaning that short of a divorce, which will mean a messy, expensive, scandalous, long-suffering ordeal, you and I *are* wed." Perhaps it was time to try a different tactic to usher in her revenge. "We either find a way to get along while in London or we remove to your country estate in Essex, where we'll have more room to divide the living space."

He frowned, and those sensual lips pulled downward. Would they be soft or firm, commanding or yielding if she were to kiss him? "Why are you familiar with where I live?"

Had he not listened to anything she'd said? Stamping a bare foot in annoyance, she huffed again. "I met my best friend at that estate, for my brother's property abuts yours."

A muscle in his cheek twitched. For long moments, he stared at her, then he yanked off his cravat and tossed it away. His cuffs and collar soon followed, falling to the floor like spilled dollops of cream. "It matters not. None of it does." There was a certain look in his brown eyes she didn't quite trust. "I want the release more than the waves of guilt or your stubborn protests."

Drat. Drat. Drat.

Frissons of need pinwheeled through her lower belly. He meant to bed her anyway. It would be the quickest way to have him close enough to plunge her blade into his deceitful heart. Slowly, and making certain he watched, Olivia let the provocative robe fall from her shoulders. It was chilly enough in the room, for she hadn't asked Bess to fetch a footman for a fire, so her nipples hardened and thrust against the thin fabric of her night dress.

Briefly, his attention dropped to her breasts. All men were weak when it came to visual stimulation. "What are you doing?"

"Preparing." With her left hand, she pulled the couple of combs from her hair and let it tumble about her back and shoulders. After she tossed the combs onto a chair, she advanced upon him, being sure to keep the blade hidden. Physical intimacy with a man had been scarce in recent years, so anything she and the viscount exchanged tonight would be as much for her as it was him.

Why shouldn't she take surface pleasure from using him like he'd do her?

"Damn, but your boldness is refreshing even if I would have never picked you," he said with a trace of surprise in his tone, seconds before he cornered her between the hard wall of his chest and one of the bedposts.

She had enough time to stare up at him—he was quite tall—see the pain and shadows deep in the depths of his eyes and then he tugged her roughly into a loose embrace and brought his mouth crashing down on hers.

Oh, my!

Flutters filled her belly while heated need twisted down her spine. With that kiss, he wasn't playing nice. In fact, with that kiss, it felt as if he was a man who sought to outrun his demons through this medium. With a mental warning not to enjoy the embrace, for it was merely a means to an end, Olivia rested her left hand on his chest, curled her fingers slightly into the fine lawn of his shirt as he sought to deepen the kiss.

Now was her chance.

With a cry, she wrenched away and swiftly brought her knife between them. The tip of the blade scraped over his shirt-covered chest, sharp enough to cut through the fabric. "For seven years I have lived for this moment, you blackhearted bastard." Her breath came in pants as he froze, his gaze bouncing from the blade to her face. "Long have I dreamed of having you at mercy, begging for your life, which will fall on deaf ears, for I intend to carve out your cold heart for what you did to Cynthia."

A ragged gasp left his throat and his eyes widened. "How dare you say that name. What do you know of her?"

Was he daft? Could he not put together the clues? Olivia pressed the tip of the blade against his chest. A drop of blood welled around the tiny puncture. "*She* was my best friend! You killed her, so now you'll pay."

"The hell you say." For a man nearly in his cups, the viscount moved quickly. One large hand encircled her wrist before she had time to draw another breath, then he was behind her and brought that arm up her back with enough strength that her muscles protested. "Drop the damned blade."

His command rasped against the shell of her ear and brought with it a wave of awareness. When she didn't immediately follow the order, he increased the pressure on her wrist. Prickles of pain went through her arm, and when her fingers went numb, she had no choice but to relinquish her hold on the weapon. "I hate you."

The blade clattered to the hardwood floor with an overly loud echo.

"I'm not all that fond of you either," he said around a growl, while kicking the knife beneath the bed. Then he released his hold on her, and immediately, Olivia spun about to face him. "Do not try that again."

"Or what? You'll kill me too, like you did Cynthia?" To her horror, tears sprang to her eyes. She hadn't wanted to show such weakness in front of him so soon. "If it weren't for you, she would still be with us." Emotion rose in her throat. "She didn't deserve that, but you couldn't keep your hands off her or your prick in your breeches. You charmed her, had your way with her, and then once you were done, you disposed of her."

"No!" He retreated from her a few steps as if she'd struck him. "That isn't true at all. I... I loved Cynthia, have never stopped," he admitted in a choked whisper. "You are naught but a bitter harpy who thinks she knows everything, and since you wish to make my life miserable, I shall do the same for yours. Misery, after all, loves company, so this Christmastide will wither with it."

Without giving her the chance for a rebuttal, he strode across the room, wrenched open the door and then stormed into the corridor beyond, being sure to slam the panel behind him.

For a few seconds, Olivia stared at the empty space he'd previously occupied, then with a cry of anguish and tears running down her cheeks, she flung herself onto the bed and sobbed out her grief and anger.

It was a wedding night to remember, indeed, but for all the wrong reasons.

Chapter Five

December 18, 1817
Ashbury House
Manchester Square
London, England

Thomas came awake to the odd feeling of being watched. And to a wretched, pounding headache. When he opened his eyes, he found his wife's dog staring at him from the chair beside his bed, those beady black eyes judging, his black whiskers quivering, and that pointy snout ready to wrap his jaws around whatever portion of Thomas' anatomy he could find.

"Go 'way," he mumbled before burying his face into his pillow. But the feeling didn't cease. With a sigh, he once more lifted his head. The damned dog was still there, and this time he uttered a soft "woof" in apparent welcome or disdain. Groaning, for any sound made the drums in his head beat ever louder, he stared at the rust-colored beast. "You look like a damned, fluffy rat."

Who bears my name.

Why would someone name their fluffball of a canine after him? He rolled onto his side facing the dog, who stared back with what looked like a mixture of curiosity and pity. If dogs could show such emotions. From the light streaming in from the windows of his bedroom along with the seemingly never-ending chiming of the longcase clock in the corridor proclaiming the noon hour, he had been abed for quite a long time.

Memories came slowly trickling back to him from last night containing knives and kisses. What the devil did it mean? And they hadn't been very good kisses, either. Barely had he started to kiss her than she'd tried to stab him. Despite the pain in his head from far too many drinks before he'd finally retired, he recalled going to his wife's bedchamber with the intent to bed her for no other reason than he'd wished to pursue a physical release.

Hellfire and damnation.

Accusations from them both flew through his cluttered brain, and a rushed profession that he had loved Cynthia. No other memories came to light, but he supposed what he had was enough. He'd made a bloody fool of himself on his wedding night, had thought he might bed her regardless of their union being in name only because he'd been nearly out of his mind with anger, grief, and arousal.

Like an idiot.

Yet what she'd said to him continued to haunt him. She'd accused him of killing Cynthia, which is what precipitated her revenge. Rolling onto his back, he quickly examined his chest where the tip of her blade had cut him. Yes, there was the wound, scabbed over with a trace of dried blood still evident. So he hadn't dreamed that particular scenario. Where the devil had she come by a dagger? When the dog bounced onto the bedside table, knocking a sketchpad, pencil nub and an empty brandy glass to the floor, Thomas sighed. He peered at the fluffy menace, took in the dog's tongue hanging out one side of his pointy little mouth, and sighed again.

"Fine. You have my permission to come onto the bed." Just this once, and he would never tell… What was his wife's name? Damn, but those memories were tricky business. He rubbed a hand along the side of his face as the dog bounded onto his pillow then proceeded to twirl around in maddening circles on the side of the bed next to him. Ah, yes. Olivia something. It had a pretty ring to it. He frowned at the dog. "Olivia Rose." When the fluffy canine gave a low bark and wagged his curly tail, Thomas couldn't help but snicker. "Well, you aren't stupid, for you know your mistress, but why does she think I'm a murderer?"

The dog sat on his haunches and stared at Thomas as if to say, "Think it through, man."

Christ, it hurt to think or keep his eyes open. Though the December sunshine wasn't strong, it was the damn glare that almost had his head splitting open. And the effort was too much for him. What he needed right now was answers. She'd said Cynthia had been her best friend, but never in his time with Cynthia had she ever mentioned a redhaired girl by the name of Olivia. What sort of stories had she heard in Essex?

And more to the point, was that what everyone in the country assumed? That he'd killed her to keep their relationship quiet?

"Let us hope your mistress is awake," he told the dog, and when he struggled into a sitting position and swung his legs over the side of the bed, he groaned again from the pain in his head. The dog trotted over the rumpled bedclothes to his side, put a tiny paw on his thigh, and let out another soft bark. "If she isn't, I suppose you need to go outside and do the necessary." It wasn't a question.

The dog wagged his tail and looked expectantly at him.

Damn it all to hell.

Standing was a small battle, and once he'd done the necessary behind his privacy screen, followed by a bout of retching, he brushed his teeth, cleaned up with a sponge and a bit of finely milled soap, and when the choice of attire stymied him, Thomas merely shucked into a pair of buff-colored breeches he found flung over the back of a chair in the adjoining dressing room. No doubt his valet was at luncheon with the rest of the staff. No need to bother him. It was too much effort to locate a shirt, so he went without. "Come on, you fluffy rat." When he wrenched open the door and went into the corridor, the dog bounded off the bed, flew over the floor, and then darted from the room. He ran with abandon into the hall, but instead of going toward his mistress' suite, the dog pelted to the stairs and descended at a reckless pace. Thomas shook his head. "Good luck. Perhaps Wallace will let you out."

Ignoring the headache, he kept one hand on the wall as he followed the corridor to the opposite end. Not wishing to give her warning in which she might find an opportunity to throw her blade at him, he pressed the brass handle. It wasn't locked, so when the door swung open on silent hinges, he let himself into the apartment and just as softly closed the panel behind him.

He breathed a sigh of relief when he didn't see a maid. As quietly as he could, Thomas padded over the floor toward the bed and was immediately reminded of his mother, for she'd decorated this suite years ago. It hadn't been used in an age, but knowing his wife now occupied the space made him hope that his mother might approve, for all she'd ever wanted him to do was marry and be happy.

Of course, she'd never known that he'd given away his heart to a maid in his father's employ and she certainly hadn't borne witness to him being forced into a loveless union with a woman who was nothing more than a stranger, her hand won at a faro table, but that was beside the point. Too bad he didn't have access to her council now when everything was so terribly convoluted, and he wanted nothing more than to bury himself in the past.

That was one luxury not afforded to him.

Then he paused at the edge of the bed to find his wife lying on her stomach with a pillow tucked beneath her head and one leg crooked at the knee. She was completely dead to the world, perhaps exhausted after everything that had happened yesterday. Still clad in the frothy, silken creation from last night, the hem had been hitched up her legs, revealing trim ankles, shapely calves, and a hint of luscious thighs. A faint scent of lilacs wafted to his nose, and he remembered that from their brief kiss from the night before.

"Olivia?" Granted, the inquiry came out of his mouth in a barely audible whisper, but the woman on the bed didn't stir. If they hadn't both been fueled by anger last night or perhaps even other emotions neither of them had divulged, would there have been a different outcome? Bad kiss aside, an odd sort of swift connection had stabbed through him that he'd been too preoccupied to notice at the time.

Possibly, but he hadn't changed his mind about allowing her access to his heart even if she was his legal wife. That didn't help the interest shivering along his shaft, for with her red hair unbound and spread about her in a scarlet cloud and the alluring sprinkle of freckles over her pale skin, he couldn't deny that she was attractive.

And he was still randy as hell.

When she didn't stir, he slipped into the bed with her, keeping to his side. Daring much, he leaned over her and pressed feather weighted kisses to her shoulders and nape. Damn, but her skin was like satin, and the heat of her called to him as strong as a siren's song. In her sleep, she uttered a few unintelligible words, and he froze, waiting to see if she would come fully awake.

When she didn't, he breathed a quick sigh of relief and continued his exploration. He trailed the fingers of one hand down her back. The silk of her gown spurred him onward. Though he had appreciated her forthrightness and penchant for plain speaking, being this close to her, feeling her skin was rather lovely too. When he bent to nuzzle the crook of her neck, he caressed the curve of her arse. What would she look like *sans* gown?

His wife murmured another few words he couldn't puzzle out. She rolled onto her side and lifted her chin. Thomas grinned. How often did she dream of just this? Settling in closer to her body, he slipped his arms around her and dared to pepper the underside of her jaw with tiny kisses. Christ, but she was a pleasing armful. His shaft agreed, for the engorged length of him pressed insistently against the front of his breeches.

If he didn't think about Cynthia or the fact this felt a bit like a betrayal of her memory, he could enjoy himself. And why shouldn't he? Love wasn't needed for a sweaty coupling that meant nothing. Soon enough, their limbs tangled together. He pulled her closer with a hand on her rear as he claimed her lips with his. When she kissed him back with a subtle sound of pleasure in her throat, some of his control skittered away.

Those two pieces of flesh cradled his as she drew a hand down the length of his back. Soft as a petal but creating chaos in his blood, those lips were highly craveable, and he continued to kiss her as if he had all the time in the world, as if he had every right to be in her bed. Suddenly, he needed more. When he dared to cup one of her breasts, he stifled a groan for the warm, soft globe fit his palm as if made for him. All too soon, the nipple hardened from his manipulation, and as she moaned, he took full advantage, encouraged her lips to part, and he deepened the embrace by seeking out her tongue with his. Curiosity battled with control as well as conscience, but he didn't stop.

Especially not when she scuttled ever closer, matching him stroke for stroke, kissing him back as if she hadn't been with a man so intimately in a lifetime. The pad of his thumb worried her nipple and she moaned again, squirmed against him, stretched along the length of his body like a cat. Need pulsed through his engorged shaft.

Thomas bent his head, took the nipple into his mouth through the thin fabric of her night dress. The difference of textures between the slippery silk, the slightly scratchy lace, and the pebbled surface of the nipple became an erotic delight and one he chased with enthusiasm. To be able to taste her, properly explore her naked form would have been the ideal way to ward off the typical maudlin thoughts.

Another pass of her nipple with his thumb provoked a whimpering sort of moan from her. What would set her aflame? Were the rumors about her true and she was little better than a courtesan? Would her reputation put a black mark against his name?

The tiny distraction proved the end of his impromptu seduction, for Olivia came awake in his arms with a start. Before he could draw another breath, that damned dagger point was against his heart, and once more the blade scratched his skin as she tipped him onto his back.

"What is the meaning of this trespass?" She knelt at his side, and her hand never wavered. The hard points of her nipples showed through the thin silk, to only enhance the tension of the moment.

"You are my wife." Why did he keep coming back to that fact? It literally had no bearing in the moment, for he would never take a woman against her will.

One of her red eyebrows rose in challenge. "In name only, remember."

As if he could forget that charged nuptial ceremony yesterday. "Fine, then I need answers." If he kept her talking, perhaps she wouldn't realize he sported quite the cockstand.

"In how to arouse a woman?" She softly clicked her tongue. "In that, you'll need to do better. It felt as if I were being teased by a rabbit."

Heat crept up his neck, and he was all too conscious of the blade against his naked chest. "You didn't seem to have an issue with it just now. In fact, you were kissing me back quite handily." Which only made her insistence that the union be in name only all the more interesting. Only time would tell where things went from here.

At least she had the grace to blush. "It is not a sin to enjoy the physical side of a relationship." She met his gaze with her clear gray eyes. "However, I swear I will cut out your damned heart if you think to trifle with me."

For the space of a few heartbeats, he remained still beneath her. Not because he was frightened of her blade—he knew he could easily disarm her again—but because part of him wished to know how she felt about the marriage and what her plans were to survive it.

With him.

"Regardless of how or why we were wed, there are responsibilities here. And I will eventually need an heir." The word stuck in his throat, for he'd nearly had that with Cynthia. "Much later," he managed to gasp, for in this moment, he didn't believe he could go through that again for obvious reasons. "I have never claimed a woman against her will, and that won't start with you." Damn, but his head pounded now that he wasn't distracted with other more delicious endeavors.

"At least you are honest. I can see that in your eyes." She lifted the dagger point from his skin. Thomas relaxed with a quick sigh. "We will need to know each other better before any of *that* is allowed or even encouraged."

"In this I agree." There would be a reprieve of sorts. *Thank God.*

Olivia nodded. "Please ask your questions. I will try to answer as honestly as I can."

"Very well." Trying not to be overly distracted by her body only made him notice her more, and that had annoyance roiling through his chest. "Where did you come by the notion that I killed Cynthia?" Perhaps he had, in a roundabout way, but that was beside the point.

"Hmm." When she cocked her head, the red waterfall of her hair tumbled over a shoulder to hide one of her luscious breasts. "Her mother summoned me when Cynthia lay dying." The delicate tendons of her throat worked with a hard swallow. "I came as quickly as I could but was too late. They wouldn't let me see her, but I knew she'd been with you throughout the year..." Her voice broke.

"And you assumed, jumped to a wild conclusion." His own throat felt raw. "You, ah, don't know to this day *how* she died?" It was inconceivable to him, but in a way, he was grateful everyone involved in that horrid day had kept the secret as he'd asked.

"No." Her chin wobbled, but she glared at him. "Do you?"

"Yes." It was something he couldn't escape from. Unable to see the judgment in her eyes, Thomas scrambled off the bed. He padded over the floor to one of the windows, watched the outside world as clouds rolled in to block out the sun. "Cynthia was with child," he finally said in a low voice graveled with emotion.

"What?" Surprise and shock echoed in her voice and reflected in her expression. "Then… she was laboring to bring the child into the world when she perished?"

"Yes." A wave of grief welled into his chest that he hadn't expected. Thomas fought against the memories, the feelings as best he could. "We were secretly engaged." There was no harm in telling the tale except it awakened the emotions that were never far from the surface.

The dagger fell from her lax fingers to the counterpane. "You were engaged." It wasn't a question.

"Yes."

"To Cynthia." Clearly, she didn't believe it and sounded like a rather dull parrot.

"I was." He tried swallowing down the lump in his throat with little success. "She and I were in love. Scandalously so, but were forced to hide it due to my father's opposition."

Olivia raked the fingers of one hand through her mass of hair. "Cynthia never told me any of it beyond finally saying who it was that had managed to turn her head." Hurt sounded in her tones. "I would have been so happy for her."

Some of her sadness connected with his, and in that one moment, they had something in common—shared grief. "It had to be a secret. My father was rather opinionated about me marrying beneath my class."

"I can understand that. Not that I condone such thinking, but I understand it." Then her lips turned down in a frown, and he couldn't stop staring at those two, full pieces of flesh that had cradled his. "Would you have married her regardless?"

"Oh, yes." Of that he had no doubt. "We had planned to run away in order to do the deed." He cleared his throat when emotions threatened to overtake him again. "I loved her with my whole heart." When that organ hurt, he rubbed a hand on his chest above it. "I so wanted that babe—my own little family," he finished in a choked whisper with a trace of tears in his eyes, so he kept his back to her lest she make jest of him.

For long moments, Olivia remained silent. "You weren't good enough for her."

"Oh, don't I know it? She had more honor and integrity and bravery in her little finger than I've managed to find in a lifetime. My father maintained she wasn't good enough for me, though, but I didn't care. She was my everything." He turned about in time to see another round of surprise flit over her face.

"I'm sorry."

"Thank you." For the moment, he refused to let on that the child lived and was quite near. The admission he had given her was all too much. Already, his emotions were ready to shatter. They pulsed to the same rhythm of his head. "I was there, in that room, Olivia." He rather enjoyed the sound of her name. "When Cynthia breathed her last, I was there, and I…"

"Yes?" So many emotions crowded her eyes he couldn't separate them.

"When I say I cannot go through such again, that I am not strong enough, I'm not lying. And I certainly cannot give you my heart." A sob welled up and he did his best to tamp it down. "My heart died with her, so *our* union will never be one of love."

How could it when he could barely survive day to day without thinking about Cynthia?

"I understand." That didn't prevent tears from pooling in her expressive eyes. "I suppose it *would* be bad form to kill you now after you've shared your story. Unless you're lying…"

"I am not." His voice was ragged even to his own ears. "Yet you and I *are* married."

"Under duress." She frowned, and once more his attention drifted to her mouth. "It is a fact neither of us can escape."

"Somehow, that doesn't matter. What is done is done." They were trapped quite neatly thanks to Mrs. Dove-Lyon. "Perhaps we should call a truce through Twelfth Night." Where the devil had that come from?

"That might be best. If we are to have peace, both of us need to work toward that goal." A sigh issued from her that sounded long-suffering. "You are broken, and I am nothing except scandalous. A fine pair we make indeed." A shrug lifted her shoulders, temporarily pulled the fabric of her night wear tight over her breasts. "*Is* ours a marriage in name only then?"

Far too many deep questions while his head pounded. "It has to be thus," he agreed in a low voice. "At least until we can come to a different understanding."

She nodded. "No toss in the sheets merely for the pleasure of it?" Was that a trace of disappointment in her voice?

How interesting, and it fired his curiosity. "We shall take one day at a time."

"It is the best we can do, for you and I are strangers." For long moments, she stared at him with speculation in her clear gray eyes. "Did you simply stop living once Cynthia died?"

Dear God, would the questions never end? But Thomas nodded. "I suppose I did." He cocked an eyebrow. What was good for the goose was good for the gander. "Just as you wasted those same years plotting your revenge against me."

"Well." A blush stained her cheeks that almost matched her hair in color. "Perhaps I still do want that."

"Even after you just said you probably shouldn't kill me? Why?" Truly, she was a riddle.

"You remain an arse who wouldn't look past Conor's debt." But a tiny smile curved her lips that he suddenly found himself wanting to provoke more of from her. "Although, my brother is an arse as well, so perhaps I won't try to put an end to your life so hard."

An unexpected chuckle left his throat. "I'll take that for the blessing it is meant to be and leave you to your day."

She climbed off the bed after him as he headed toward the door. "Where will you be?"

"It is information you are not privy to." If the rain held off, he would go to Hyde Park for a chance to glimpse his child as per usual.

That part of his heart he wasn't willing to open yet to strangers.

Chapter Six

December 19, 1817

Olivia hadn't seen her husband since yesterday morning when he'd come in and had awakened her with kisses and caresses. It had been a spectacular way to greet the day, and although she'd once more held her dagger at his heart, the overwhelming desire to carve that organ from his chest had dimmed.

For far too many years, she'd pushed everything aside as she'd planned and plotted her revenge. Now that she'd been given that chance twice and hadn't been able to follow through, she was suddenly left bereft of purpose. Yes, she was still racked with grief from losing her best friend, but seven years was a long time to mourn, and part of her niggled at her to remember that life should be lived to the fullest.

Wouldn't that be the best way to honor Cynthia? Perhaps if a child resulted from this union—a female child—they could both be persuaded to name her after the woman who had inadvertently brought them together.

That brought a different welling of tears to her eyes, which she rapidly blinked away lest the servants assume Ashbury was naught but an ogre. She'd had that tiny little dream in her grasp once, but it had been lost far too soon. Like her husband, she couldn't help but wonder if she was strong enough to take on that hope again.

In this moment, she didn't know, and it didn't matter besides. They had agreed their marriage would be in name only for a while. It was better that way, for as soon as carnal pleasures were introduced, she had the tendency to lose her common sense as well as her control. It would be far too disastrous to do both while trapped in a union she hadn't wanted in the first place. One never knew what a man would think up to keep a woman beneath his thumb, and weren't they all liars besides?

No matter her doubts, the viscount was her husband, and this was her lot. None of that discounted the fact she was both annoyed and confused by him. Thomas had seemed genuinely upset when he'd talked of Cynthia yesterday and drat if the way he'd woken her wasn't the height of romantic.

If she wasn't careful, she might develop a fondness for him, and that was simply far too foreign after years spent hating him sight unseen. He had the potential to be pleasant if he would let himself.

Why was marriage such a puzzle to be solved?

"Do you have a thought on which dress you would like to wear today, my lady?"

The sound of Bess' voice broke into Olivia's musings. She sighed. "Not particularly. Whatever you think is good enough. I'll probably just trail about the house and explore." She needed to do more than sit around knitting. Though the product of that hobby was lovely, she needed something else to occupy her mind.

"Then I'll pull out one of your older dresses. Since you had the modiste in yesterday, hopefully the new clothing you ordered will arrive before Christmastide."

"That is the thought, especially since Conor let me have my pick from the bolts of fabric sitting in the warehouse. That should expedite the process." No doubt her brother was suffering from guilt, and since the goods weren't selling as quickly, she'd wanted to make use of them, to show them off if she were forced to be in society on the off chance someone would wish to know where the eye-catching fabric came from.

Would her husband applaud her creativity and thriftiness?

In short order, Olivia was garbed in a day dress of navy wool with the veriest hint of silver embroidery about the rounded neckline and the wrists of the long sleeves. A black braided cord emphasized her waist, and she'd donned black half boots, for it was a chilly day with rain in the offing. If fate were kind, there might be snow soon or ice on the Serpentine that would allow skating in the shallower parts. That was one activity she adored while in London during the winter. Yes, she could indulge in the country, but there was something about the happy, calling crowds and the twinkling lights in Hyde Park that was particularly magical.

"If you could send the black bonnet and cloak down to Wallace? No doubt Kip will need to be walked later, and I might fancy exploring the square a bit before coming back in." The poor butler had taken care of the dog yesterday morning when she'd been involved with the viscount, and she didn't want that to become a habit. Kip was her responsibility, and if he continued to annoy her husband, then all would be well.

"Of course, my lady." Bess offered a smile. "Enjoy your day."

"I will certainly try." She frowned. Though not being familiar with her husband's moods, that might take more than two days. Surely, he didn't mope about the townhouse like a maudlin ghost. "Oh, and bring my knitting basket down to the drawing room. It's chilly enough that having the blanket I'm currently working on will be most welcome." For that matter, how did Thomas like spending his leisure? It was something she would like to discover and soon, merely to have a conversational topic.

"I will do it right now."

"Thank you." It was exceedingly odd having to remember that there were a bevy of servants willing to attend to her every need. There was a staff at her brother's townhouse, but it was much smaller, as were the contingent of servants employed at the country manor. To have such wealth that Ashbury was reported to command—as well as his contemporaries—continued to boggle her mind. "Come, Kip! We are going exploring."

The dog ran after her with a joyful bark. Thank goodness she had him; otherwise, her time as the new Lady Ashbury would be lonely indeed.

As she made her way down to the second floor, the feeling that something was missing continued to niggle at her. What was it? Pausing, she stared down at Kip, who didn't offer much in the way of prompts, but he was certainly adorable with his tongue hanging out and his whiskers twitching. She must have appeared lost, for Wallace met her in the corridor with a frown.

"Is something amiss, my lady?"

"Oh." How silly of her. "Not that I can see. However, it doesn't appear this townhouse is equipped to celebrate Christmastide."

"That is correct, my lady." His shrug was as elegant as if he were employed by a duke or king. "Lord Ashbury has passed many such holidays without fanfare." He glanced at Kip, but she couldn't decide if the butler was happy or annoyed to see the dog.

"Then there are no decorations stored within this house?" How exceedingly odd.

"I don't believe so." An expression of surprise crossed his face. "Perhaps there are some boxes of such in the manor house, but not here. The viscount hasn't apparently felt festive for some years."

"Ah." No doubt he thought while he struggled with grief, he couldn't allow himself to enjoy anything else. How well she knew that feeling. "I'm sorry to hear that." She frowned. "Does the staff wish to decorate, though?"

"Of course, my lady. We all remember how it used to be with the viscount, how he usually celebrated when his parents were alive, both here and in the country." The man paused, confliction in his expression. "However, we haven't done so out of respect for him. For whatever reason, he has withdrawn into himself. When he is not closeted away in his study, he spends his time at his clubs."

That was not a productive life, and neither would it bring him happiness or fulfillment. "Wallace, I realize *you* won't step out of your place, but please secure *me* the various greenery and swags we will need for a lovely Christmastide season." She gave him an encouraging smile. "We needn't host a ball or something grand like that, but we *can* mark the season and possibly help Ashbury to remember there is life beyond what haunts him."

And in the process, perhaps she could remember that as well.

The older man's eyebrows soared into his wispy white hair line. "Lord Ashbury won't be pleased."

"No doubt he will not, but I will deflect his ire onto myself. Since I have already incurred his wrath by bringing a dog into his home, this shouldn't be so difficult to overcome. I am his viscountess, and *I* would like to see greenery in this house, smell the scents, see the candlelight sparkle off tin bells and glass balls. Beyond that, it encourages goodwill with the staff." Then she shrugged and met the older man's faded blue eyes. "He cannot go on as before; none of us can. While change is difficult at first, it is usually good for the soul."

"I hope you are right."

So do I, but she didn't think Ashbury was a violent man, and neither did he have a monstrous temper. He was merely racked with anger and guilt over an unkind fate. When Kip uttered a bark, no doubt to spur her into motion, she shushed him. "Speaking of the viscount, where is he?"

"I would have no idea, my lady. He rarely tells me his destination when he leaves the house."

Despite her own anger over the past as well as for the situation and the new role she'd been forced to assume, a tiny tremble moved through her heart, for he was struggling just as much. The only difference being her grief came out in the need for revenge while he didn't have an outlet. "I will find him. Where does he spend most of his time outside the house?"

A look of confusion crept over the butler's face. "A few times a week, if the weather is fine, he enjoys going to Hyde Park. Sometimes he walks for the exercise, but at others, he sits on a bench or a stone wall near the water and does nothing at all." He tugged on the knot of his cravat. "Er, at least that is what his drivers have always reported."

Ah, that was how he'd kept fit. An image of his naked chest jumped into her mind's eye. The mat of blond curls had covered that area and then tapered into a thin ribbon down his mostly flat abdomen before disappearing beneath his breeches. Oh, how she'd ached to explore that tempting line! "I see." How very interesting and quite intriguing. She quite ignored the heat in her cheeks. "Inform me when the greenery arrives. Tomorrow I will go shopping for decorations, baubles, and ribbons." After all, she had a monthly allowance to use however she wished, with no opposition from her husband. "Everyone is welcome to help me decorate the rooms if they would like."

"Of course, my lady." The butler gave her a genuine smile. "We would all enjoy that."

"So would I." Perhaps it would make her feel more at home. She waved as the butler continued along the corridor. If the viscount was out of the house just now, she could discover clues that might offer insight into him as a person. Since the study was a favorite room of his, she would start there. "Come along, Kip. We have some investigating to do."

The dog trotted after her without comment, but he did nip at the hem of her dress once, and tumbled down a few steps at the bottom of the staircase as they gained the ground floor. The poor dear's little legs just weren't long enough to account for the speed he wanted.

As soon as Olivia opened the study door, Thomas' scent teased her nose. Whatever else the man was, he smelled heavenly. Sandalwood, citrus, and subtle notes of leather teased her olfactory senses. The room itself fairly screamed his presence, and she stood there basking in that essence for the space of a few heartbeats. Cherrywood furniture, heavy maroon draperies and rugs reflecting those shades filled the room. A few shelves with books lined two walls, the subjects of which varied from poetry, gardening, drawing, and political discourse. None of that would offer a clear clue, but she found his tastes interesting, nonetheless.

Kip immediately hopped onto a low settee off to one side and laid down. The dog wasn't picky at where he napped, but he watched her as she sat in a buttery soft leather chair behind the massive desk.

Ledgers were stacked neatly in one corner. Envelopes lay in two orderly piles—one opened and one for letters that hadn't been. Pen and inkwell were placed in the middle just so. A handsome decanter of leaded crystal occupied another corner with a tawny colored-liquor inside, no doubt brandy. A glass in the same style rested beside it. Truly, it was a tidy desk, but did it reflect his inner soul? His inner thoughts?

Did he feel confused or adrift as she did most of the time?

There was no way of knowing, so the search would continue. Olivia opened one of the drawers. She particularly admired the knobs of tortoiseshell. Several leatherbound notebooks met her gaze. They were stacked inside in a neat tower, and a set of charcoals rested beside them as if an artist occupied the space. Intrigued, she pulled out one of the books, undid the leather ties, and then opened it. "Oh!" Not a notebook at all but a sketchbook!

And from the looks of it, this was the most recent of the stack, for most of the pages were blank, but the first ones contained drawings—caricatures really—each done with great skill and attention to detail. Immediately, she recognized most of the men depicted in the pages, and what was more, the style was all too familiar.

"Where have I seen you before?" she asked of the drawings, then she sucked in a breath, for she *knew*. Viscount Ashbury was the political artist whose work landed in various newspapers around London! "Oh, dear heavens, this is a marvelous find!" Not only did it mean the viscount had a sense of humor, but he also didn't give out respect just because men in power felt they deserved it.

With excitement twisting up her spine, Olivia removed another sketchbook from the bottom of the stack. Every page in this one was full; the style just as vivid but not the caricatures of the other book. Amidst the pages were portraits, some with the subject looking directly at the artist and some not. Still other drawings were of views of London and even more from the countryside, but there was a clear theme to most of them—Cynthia. She stared back at Olivia from multiple pages; he'd captured her flawlessly. Her essence leapt from the pages in shades of charcoal.

"My, my, Ashbury, you have quite the talent." Each drawing was more visually stunning than the last. Such care and detail were included on every page that she was left breathless at some of them. There was a couple she didn't know but assumed were his parents since the father had some of the same features that Thomas had. In the drawings of Cynthia, he'd managed to capture her in time. Some were frivolous, some serious, some all too risqué, but there was no doubt the happiness in her eyes and smile.

Truly, she had been very much in love with the viscount, which made his stunted feelings and the shadows in his eyes all the more devastating. Perhaps he didn't know how to release those emotions and make room for new ones.

Did I judge him too harshly?

A whine from Kip alerted her to potential intrusion then the viscount was there in the open door with an expression like a thunderstorm.

"What the hell are you doing in here?" The inquiry echoed in the small space.

Kip, coward that he was, bolted from the room with a sharp bark of exception.

Oh, dear. That's what I get for sneaking through forbidden places. "I..." Slowly, Olivia stood as she searched her mind for words that might calm him, for she hadn't seen him so incensed, but then, she'd only known him two days. "I wanted to learn more about you—"

"So you went where you shouldn't? Got into my private, personal things?"

Well, there was no covering her tracks now since the sketchbooks lay open on the desk. "I did, and what's more, I learned one of your secrets." Which was still amazing. "You are the political artist of the newspaper. The one who pokes fun at everyone regardless of what side of an issue they're on."

When he didn't say anything, she grinned.

"You are also a fantastic artist in your own right, and I am in awe at your talent."

Shock lined his face for the space of a breath, but then that emotion fell to anger as he swiftly came around the desk, gathered the sketchbooks, stuffed them back in the drawer, and slammed it shut. The sound echoed in the room, but it was his glare that sent cold foreboding circling through her belly. "That was supposed to be private."

"While I understand that, they are lovely. You managed to capture her quite effortlessly. I..." She cleared her throat, for suddenly too many emotions crowded it. "Almost for a moment I could believe she was still with us."

"Thank you." The same emotions passed over his face and collected in his eyes as he fought for control. "It doesn't matter now. I really should burn those books."

"No!" Daring much, Olivia laid a hand on his arm. The muscles went taut beneath her fingertips. "Please don't. It is good to remember, and it *does* matter, Thomas." Saying his name aloud was rather lovely too. "You should frame a couple of the best ones. In an effort not to forget her, if you truly loved her."

For one terrible second, his chin trembled, and that tiny tell endeared him to her more than weeks of conversation. "It isn't your business," he said in a low, growling voice as he loomed over her.

Then her tendency toward annoyance got the better of her, for it was a difficult habit to break. "It *is* because you are my *husband*—for better or worse—and you are haunted. How can we build anything upon that shaky foundation?" When tears welled in her eyes, she rapidly tried to blink them away. "You aren't the only one who misses her."

"I was the one who loved her!"

"Do you not believe there are other kinds of love beyond romantic?" If her voice rose with the inquiry, she couldn't help it. "Perhaps it will help us both with our grief if we openly talk about her, share our memories, keep her presence alive in our hearts instead of trying to avoid everything about her."

"Why?" He shook his head. "So you can carve me up like a kitchen ham?" Bitterness rode on those words, and she hated herself in that moment.

"I..." Had her purpose changed?

The viscount advanced on her, trapped her between him and the desk which pressed against her buttocks. "I don't need to grieve."

"Why?" She continued to push. "It is not weakness to shed tears or mourn someone's passing."

A muscle ticced in his cheek. "I am afraid... that if I let myself grieve, it will be all too final and then, little by little, I'll forget her."

"That is why you have the drawings." When he didn't answer, she blew out a breath. "You are nearly breaking from it now, Ashbury. So let it go. Cynthia is gone, has been gone for years now. She isn't coming back." For her own sanity, Olivia needed to remember that as well.

"I can't!" He raked the fingers of one hand through his hair. "It is my prerogative—"

"It will be your destruction," she said in a lower voice. The scent of him, the heat radiating off his body all worked to distract her from the conversation. His presence was too much, too big, too angry to ignore but if he wouldn't let her in, she couldn't help him.

And she needed to learn the lesson too.

"You know nothing of it."

"Then tell me! Rail at me if you need to, but at least purge yourself of the pent-up feelings so you can begin moving forward. You still have much living to do."

He scoffed. "And let you see me shatter?"

"If you do, I wouldn't feel so alone and lost," she admitted in a barely audible tone.

For long moments he stared at her. After that, she was never sure who moved first, but suddenly she was in his arms and his lips were on hers. A different energy propelled them together, a frantic need, a bond in grief that fueled the kiss.

Seconds later, he lifted her up, then set her arse on the desk, and still he kissed her as if she held the last bit of air and the world was ending. He cupped her cheeks, held her stationary while he explored every centimeter of her mouth, and when she paused for the pedestrian reason of breathing, he took full advantage and deepened the embrace. As his tongue touched hers, dared her to fence with his, she complied immediately with a sigh and flutters in her lower belly.

Surprise gave way to pleasure with each stroke of her tongue against his. With every nip and nibble, she shivered from the delicious eroticism of the embrace, for it was all too lovely to feel that heat, that connection, to feel wanted again by a man. Over and over, Olivia returned his kisses, gave as much as she took.

"Hold." Ashbury wrenched away, his brown eyes darkened to the hue of strong tea as he held her gaze. "We need more room." Before she could wonder about what he meant, he'd swept the ledgers, letters, and books from the desk; they made a dull thud upon the carpet as they fell. The mostly empty decanter of brandy and the glass were thrust to one side and out of the way. "Much better." Then he laid her back on the desk and followed her down while he stood between her naturally splayed legs.

"Merciful heavens," she whispered seconds before he claimed her mouth again and took full possession. There was no doubt in her mind he was impressive and that he'd chosen to channel his emotions into something more productive and oh so satisfying.

A grunt escaped him, and it seemed as if his hands were everywhere at once. It took little time or effort for him to tug down the bodice of her dress and bare her breasts. With a moan of anticipation, she snaked a hand about his nape and guided his mouth to a hardened, aching nipple.

"Dear God, it has been too long..." The rest of her words were swallowed up by a sigh as he sucked that tip into the warm cavern of his mouth and worried it with his tongue.

He chuckled, then released the nipple. Immediately, the sharp contrast of the cool air on the damp tip had her squirming. "In this, I fully agree with you." Ashbury took that breast in his hand, kneading it, manipulating it, rolling the bud while he took the other one into his mouth.

Awash on a sea of pleasure that streaked from her breasts into her core, Olivia struggled to do something—anything—besides lay there. She buried her fingers through his thick hair, lifted her hips and wriggled them in an effort to feel the evidence of his desire at her center, and he was *quite* aroused. Shivery need climbed her spine. What would it take for him to couple with her right here?

He continued to play at her breasts, tease her nipples while lovely pressure built and stacked in her core. Like a man who suddenly remembered how wonderful it could be to enter into a physical relationship with a woman, he kept her writhing beneath him while low moans issued from her throat, and she clung to his shoulders in an effort to stay fairly upright.

But he wasn't nearly done with her. As he dragged his lips along the side of her neck, he glided a hand beneath her skirting. Soon enough, those talented fingers were between her thighs, furrowing through the curls there until he parted her flesh and encouraged the bud at her center out of hiding.

"Ashbury…" The words of caution she meant to say flew right out of her brain the second he strummed his fingers over that pearl. "Mmm, yes, just there."

"I adore a woman who knows exactly how she likes to be pleasured," he murmured against the underside of her jaw, while continuing to experiment with varying degrees of pressure and friction.

"Well, I like many things having to do with physical relations," she managed to gasp out as her hold on sanity rapidly slipped away. Far too primed after their verbal sparring and the brief kisses and caresses given yesterday morning, her body shook with the need to shatter.

"So tempting…" He returned to suckle at a breast while increasing his friction to that bundle of nerves at her center. Around and around his tongue went about her nipple and his finger followed the same pattern. When he lightly bit the nipple, he gave the pearl a little squeeze, and she nearly vaulted off the desk.

"Oh, oh, yes, just a bit more…" There was no shame in begging, for this moment belonged solely to them and the raw need for release.

"Damn, but I want to ravish you right here, want to hear you scream." Then another kiss stopped the flow of words, and his fingers created magic between her thighs.

She fell back onto her elbows and arched her back. "There is nothing to stop you, Ashbury." The words were faint and breathless, for she was very nearly there. With another stroke of his finger, she was hurled over the edge into bliss. "Thomas!" The shout of his name was louder than she'd intended, but in that moment she didn't care. Every nerve ending in her body tingled with pleasure. Heat rolled over her as she collapsed onto the desk while contractions fluttered through her core. "Please, finish me," she gasped out.

"Damn." Suddenly, he backed away, staring at her as if he couldn't believe what he'd just done. "I can't…" The shadows were once more in his eyes. "This changes nothing within our relationship." Before she could say anything, the viscount had quit the room, and the soft snick of the door closing echoed in her ears.

"Well, drat." With a sigh and an unfilled feeling circling through her body, Olivia struggled into a seated position. That would have been the truth except this session had changed everything slightly. She was far too intrigued by him and wanted to help him heal, and perhaps in the process, heal herself.

Damn his eyes.

Chapter Seven

What the hell is wrong with me?

Thomas frowned as he did a quick tour of the townhouse. It was time for tea, and he thought that perhaps Olivia might wish to join him so he could apologize for what happened in his study. To come the crab over her finding his private drawings had been bad enough, but then for him to violate her as if she were little better than a courtesan? On his desk no less? That was outside of enough.

Yet in a different part of his brain, he remained a bit smug. It wasn't as if he'd forced himself on his wife; she'd returned those kisses with just as much enthusiasm and passion and she could have begged off at any time. Instead, she'd urged him onward, and had been quite vocal about it, especially when she'd found bliss.

Interesting, that, to have a wife who wasn't afraid or disgusted by carnal play. For far too long, he'd assumed that when he did marry to do his duty by his title, his choice of mate would be limited to an innocent, starry-eyed chit just making her Come Out, a woman too dim to have heard the rumors about him, or a woman who shied away from bed sport. Add to that his personal vow never to take another candidate for marriage to his bed after losing Cynthia, and he'd wished to postpone the wedded state for as long as he could.

Now that he'd been forced to wed, he was uncommonly surprised by the woman who carried the viscountess title. She was a rather interesting blend of contrasts and surprises. There was unexpected heat between them that bumped up against his control, but there was also a connection that bound them both together, a mutual bond that they had known and loved Cynthia. That shared grief was all too tempting, made him want to lower his guard and become all too vulnerable if only for a second.

As of yet, he hadn't been able to do that, to take the risk or even trust Olivia... but he was beginning to. Beyond that, she was intriguing in her own right. Despite himself, he wished to know her history, to understand her, commend her on the fierce protection she still showed for Cynthia's memory, and to ask her if she truly admired his drawings.

That brief praise from earlier had given him pause. Perhaps if she thought he had talent, he could do something with that other than enrage the political pundits and functionary men of power with his views that, at times, bordered on the salacious and slanderous.

Near the door to the drawing room, he met the butler, who was apparently making his afternoon rounds. "Say, Wallace, do you know where Lady Ashbury is at this time of day?" Heat burned up the back of his neck, for he was all too embarrassed regarding his treatment of her nearly three hours before. Did she think him a monster? A nodcock?

"I would have no idea, my lord. However, if I were to guess, she no doubt took Sir Kippington-Prestwick for a walk." The corners of that austere man's lips twitched.

Damn and blast! Why the hell did she have to name the dog after me?

"But it's spitting rain and quite chilly out there."

The butler shrugged. "As nature decrees, the bodily functions of a small canine are not dependent upon the weather."

"Of course." Thomas propped his hands on his hips. "Did she say if she planned to walk the streets of Manchester Square or merely take the canine into the garden?"

"I would rather like to think she had the garden in mind, but if the dog required more exercise, she would no doubt take him into the square." Wallace looked at him with speculation. "I suppose it would also depend on her state of mind. Walking does wonders for that."

"So I have heard." Had the butler always been so damned invested in the lives of the people he served, or had Olivia managed to make an impression on him in such a short period of time? "The daft woman should be near to freezing by now."

"Indeed, my lord." Wallace nodded. "Best go after her then, hmm?"

Now that *was* out of character for his butler. "Why?" He couldn't help but be suspicious.

"Why not?" The man affected an air of confusion. "You cannot have a viscountess if she becomes a block of ice." His lips twitched with apparent amusement.

A stab of jealousy went through Thomas' chest, for Olivia had made a fast impression on his staff, where she still held him at arm's length... except for that trespass he'd made earlier today. "Perhaps."

Wallace shifted his weight from foot to foot. "If I may speak truthfully, my lord?"

"Of course."

"Christmastide isn't the time for strife and regret and sadness. Lady Ashbury is rather—"

"Managing?" he asked with a budding grin of his own.

"No, she is—"

"Impossible?"

One of the butler's white eyebrows rose. "Rather, she is determined and headstrong." Wallace chuckled. "That isn't a bad thing, and if you listen closely to her, there is a delightful hint of an Irish lilt to her voice."

What was this, then? "Why do you say it isn't bad?" Curiosity grew strong to know the other man's insight.

For a few seconds, Wallace paused. "She is good for us all. I feel she will fix what is wrong here, put the broken things back together, bring order and happiness to our lives." He met Thomas' eyes. "We have all grown too stale and perhaps a touch jaded over the years."

Was that true? Had his mood affected his staff? Never had he thought about that before. "Perhaps we have, but I don't want to be fixed, don't need to be. There is nothing wrong with remembering." Some of his usual bitterness returned, but somehow, he didn't want to take refuge in it, for Olivia had now infiltrated his thoughts all too much.

"There is not. However, you can't continue as you are, my lord. Neither can she. You are partners. For good or for ill, you have been given each other." He shrugged. "Square with that, and finally enjoy life again."

"I shall bear that in mind." But he nodded. "I appreciate your concern for me. It is lovely, Wallace." Truly, without his loyal staff, he would have been lost to grief years ago. They kept him moving and fed him until one of his friends could take up the burden for the day. *That is no way to live.* How had he not seen it before? "My outer things, if you please."

"At once, my lord."

Together, they descended the staircase, and once in the entry hall, Wallace handed over his greatcoat and beaver felt top hat.

"Will you also ring the kitchens and order tea? No doubt Lady Ashcroft will be quite chilled upon our return." For he didn't intend to come back inside without her. There was a time and a place for obstinacy, but not at the expense of one's health.

"I would be delighted, my lord."

"Thank you." With a nod to the butler, he traversed the corridor of the lower level, ducked into the library, and then exited the house by way of the garden door in that room. Immediately, the early winter's chill went through him, and he shrugged deeper into the coat. Would they soon have snow? If so, that meant Sally would be able to skate on the ice of the Serpentine. His chest constricted. Damn, there were far too many secrets he kept. Should he share them all with his wife? Would that help matters between them?

For the time being, he had no answers.

Not seeing her in his garden, he continued onto the green space contained within the square to the rear of the buildings. Some of the trees were winter-bare, while the oaks continued to cling valiantly to most of their leaves even if they were brown. As he walked, his mind wandered once more to what had happened in his study earlier that day.

Had he gone too far? Perhaps, and he owed his wife an apology, an explanation at the very least, but damn if he hadn't enjoyed himself while discovering what she liked that would send her flying. What was more, he couldn't wait to do it all over again. In fact, it felt almost as if he'd found purpose once more, as if he had seen the way out of the darkness he'd lost himself in since meeting grief.

How the hell was that possible? It was something else he didn't know, but perhaps he needed her guidance after all.

It was a new concept having his thoughts center on himself and what he should do as well as possibly working together with his new wife instead of fixating on the past. In many ways, he couldn't change what had happened, but he could change the course of his future. That was a powerful realization.

For the first time in a long while, faint vestiges of excitement buzzed at the base of his spine. How odd, indeed. Eventually, he saw his wife walking amidst the dying winter shrubberies and hedges on a cobblestone path with the dog yapping and dancing circles about her feet. As he approached, the dulcet sound of her voice as she talked to the canine soothed his frazzled nerves, and that was truly odd as well.

"Olivia." He uttered the word far too low for her to ever hear, but apparently the rat-like dog did, for his russet ears perked, and when he caught sight of Thomas, he gave a joyful yap and then pelted over. The yapping and pawing at his boots continued until Thomas heaved a sigh and picked the fluff-ball up. A damned nuisance, but the wriggling body and tongue licking the side of his face was warm and annoyingly welcome.

"Olivia," he said softly as he approached with the dog beneath his arm.

A tiny gasp escaped her. "Ashbury." She glanced up at him, and he was taken by her looks. The red hair was like a beacon beneath her bonnet, but it was the healthy wash of golden freckles on her face that held him captive. Surprise reflected in her clear gray eyes, and suddenly, he didn't think it would be half bad to drown in those pools. "Why are you here?" Her gaze fell to Sir Kippington beneath his arm. "And why are you holding Kip? I thought you detested him?"

Of course she would focus on that. He peered at the dog, who gazed up at him with expectation in his black eyes and his pink tongue hanging out. "As a dog, I still believe he isn't worth the effort. Dogs should be strong, large, and fearless."

She snorted. "Wait until Kip gets angry. He's been known to bite ankles until the skin breaks."

"I can well imagine." He stroked the dog's head with his other gloved hand. "Be that as it may, he seems to adore you, and as long as he keeps out of my rooms, I don't mind him. Much."

"So I can see." Olivia bounced her gaze between the dog and him. "You didn't answer my initial question. Why are you here?"

He blew out a breath. "I believe I owe you an apology."

"For? There are a handful of wrongs you have perpetrated since we married."

One corner of his mouth twitched. How much was he coming to

appreciate her tart mouth? "While that may be truth, I was referring to what happened in the study earlier today."

"Why? I enjoyed myself." A shrug lifted her shoulders as she resumed her stroll. "We are wed. Even if we weren't, there is no shame in what we shared."

"No, perhaps there is not." Yet another fascinating and curious rock he wanted to overturn. Easily, he adjusted his pace to accommodate hers since she was so much shorter than he. How to broach the subject of her past? There could be no fear, for she would run with that like a dog with a bone. As Wallace said, they were partners now. He cleared his throat. "From the context of your reply, I rather doubt you are an innocent."

"Ah, and so the news of my scandals has met your ears." A trace of regret threaded through her voice. "I wondered if you'd heard."

"Indeed, but I would, ah, like to come to know you—the real you—despite what the rumors and gossips say. In doing so, I hope you would give me the same latitude." Did that mean he had given up on his vow, or was it showing growth?

Too difficult to tell.

"Why?" She frowned as she once more glanced at him with surprise in her expression.

Why indeed. "It is nearly Christmastide."

"And? I somehow doubt you have suddenly had an epiphany and wish to turn your life about merely due to an impending holiday."

"I have not." His lips twitched but he didn't give into a grin. Instead, he continued to stroke the dog's head as he walked beside his wife. "However, it felt... good to talk about Cynthia, even if it was charged with emotion—"

"More like you were discombobulated after having me spread open on your desk," she interrupted with more than a little amusement in her tone.

A chuckle escaped him as heat crept up the back of his neck. She was delightful. "I won't confirm or deny that supposition, though your charms are *quite* distracting."

"Ha!" But she grinned. "I don't believe a man has ever told me that. Most have severe aversions to the freckles. One even went so far as to tell me he'd gladly rut with me, but he would take me from behind so he wouldn't need to see them."

Thomas' lower jaw dropped. "The devil you say!" For the first time, he understood how crass and insulting men were to women. "Did you, ah, lay with him?"

"I did not."

At least there was that. He led her to a bench, and as she sat even though it was slightly wet, he settled beside her. When the rat dog shivered, Thomas opened his coat and put the animal inside on his lap. "Tell me about your history. Whatever makes you comfortable."

A quick sigh escaped her. "What if the stories aren't flattering or exciting?"

"Doesn't matter, for they are yours. They made you into the woman who tried to kill me twice."

An unexpected snicker emanated from her, and it made him stare with surprise. "Oh, Ashbury, life just didn't go as I had thought or planned, and that led to some... interesting decisions."

"Ah." He frowned. "You made use of my Christian name before. I, uh, would like it if you would again." Did that make him sound weak?

"I will." Olivia nodded. "I met Cynthia when I was eighteen and she a year younger. My parents had dreams for me to marry well; Papa's expectations and aspirations weren't mine." She frowned at the tips of her half boots. "But I loved them, so I did what I could to please them."

"I understand that all too well."

"Yes, I suppose you would." In profile, the corner of her lips turned down in a frown. "Being in society makes me anxious. Also, men don't like red hair and freckles, so I was never in the popular style. That only added to the worry and concern."

"*Some* men," he said without thought.

"Ha!" But there was a note of fond surprise in that one-word utterance that prompted his own grin. "More often than not, I liked being in the servants' hall of your father's estate in the countryside. I was accepted there more than in society, and I had a friend in Cynthia." She turned her head and gave him a soft grin. "We would have traded lives if we could have."

And I would have still married you, for if they had traded places, it would have been her he'd fallen in love with instead of Cynthia. How interesting. "Cynthia had the sweetest soul I had ever been privileged to know."

"She did." Olivia stretched out a hand, scratched at one of Kip's ears when he poked his head out from Thomas' coat. "I wanted to be like her; it didn't matter her class, there was something about her that drew people to her."

"It was one reason I fell for her," he said softly.

Olivia nodded. "After she died, I was so alone. Stunned, truly." The catch in her voice caused his heart to shiver awake. "There was a hole in my life, and then my mother died not long after that, quite unexpectedly, and my world shifted far too much. For a time, I couldn't make sense of who I was or what I needed to do."

"That is perfectly understandable. I spent much time in that place as well." It was another thing they had in common, and it wasn't as annoying as he once thought. It was nice to ... have someone to emphasize with.

For long moments, she remained quiet. Then, she sighed. "Lost and hurting, I sought companionship with a lover."

"Then the rumors are true." It wasn't a question, and there was no accusation in his tone, but he was glad it had been confirmed.

"Yes." For a fleeting second, her chin trembled. "Why is it encouraged for men to take lovers, but women are branded and ostracized for the same?"

"Society needs to hold everyone to the same standards, I agree."

"However, they don't, and people like us don't have enough power to affect that change." When she shrugged, her arm brushed his. Heated tingles ran down his arm and awoke his awareness of her. "I don't regret my past, and I refuse to feel bad when people look down on me for it. I enjoy physical relationships with men, adore bed sport."

The words, though quite scandalous, were strangely reassuring and quite stimulating. Interest shivered through his shaft, but he continued to stroke Kip's head. "I do not begrudge you the liaisons—I have had my fair share of the same over the years—but I must ask."

"Yes?" It didn't matter that the spitting rain continued or that it was quite chilly outside or even that annoyance warred with resignation in her gray eyes; he had to assuage his worries.

"Will you be faithful to me?" If their union remained in name only, it would be harsh to ask her that, for he would need to give her the same promise, so asking this now came with risks and a bit of arrogance.

She met his gaze without fear. "Will you give me the same consideration?"

Damn, but she had very nearly mirrored his own thoughts. "Of course."

"Good." His wife nodded. "As for my answer? I will. You are my husband. When I make a vow, I never break it, but if you want the couplings without the emotions, that is also quite acceptable. We both have needs. There is no shame in that either."

"No, there is not." After what happened in his study, it might become a very real possibility that they would act on the heated tension that crackled between them. "Thus far, our marriage has been a confusing issue."

"It has." A chuckle followed the words, and he rather liked the tinkling sound of that bit of laughter. "But then, life itself has been confusing for many years now." She stared into the parkland ahead of her with a faint frown tugging down the corners of her mouth.

What he wouldn't give to kiss away that emotion until she smiled again. "Olivia?"

"Hmm?"

"Have you ever been in love?" He had already shared that piece of himself with her. Perhaps it was time to learn about that side of her.

"Once." Another sigh escaped, and this time it sounded as if it had come from her toes. "A few years ago." With her gloved fingers, she toyed with a small pink, enamel rose on a silver chain that hung around her neck. "I'd met him at a rout. He was a newly minted earl. Our affair burned hot and bright; I fell hard, had my head turned after my first two lovers hadn't amounted to anything concrete."

"And?"

"I thought he loved me too, but there was no future for us. He made that perfectly clear one evening when we were alone and talking in all seriousness." Olivia glanced at him, and the sadness in her eyes stabbed through his chest. "I was nothing, I came from nothing, and he made certain to tell me that. He didn't want me for a mistress any longer, so our relationship ended far too abruptly, and he withdrew his support and protection."

Yet there were shadows in her eyes, a bit of hesitation in her voice that gave him pause. When someone edited their history, only a person who'd done the same could pick up on that fact. "What are you not telling me?" He must have held anxiety in his body, for the dog uttered a low bark and stirred restlessly in his arms. Thomas shushed it and tried to soothe the canine the best he could.

"Oh, Thomas." Much to his surprise, she stifled a sob. Emotions marched across her face he couldn't read. "I am not strong enough to reveal that part of myself in this moment."

"Fair enough." He nodded, for he held his own secret. In time, perhaps, he would share. "Do you believe you will ever love another?"

"I don't know, but it has long been a dream." A shiver racked her shoulders, and she pulled the folds of her cloak more tightly about her body. "Being in love, falling in love, opening myself up to another takes much from me, steals a piece of my soul. If I keep giving that away without a return, what will there be for me later?"

He'd not thought in terms like that before. The longer the silence stretched between them, the more he was able to see her for the woman she was—searching for belonging, needing renewed hope, to be comforted.

The same things he struggled with on a daily basis. Slowly, his views and prejudices began to shift, and it shattered him as everything began to move out of focus. "I…" What? Perhaps he should speak from a place of truth and go from there. "I am glad you are here." Damnation, but that wasn't what he'd wanted to say!

"Oh?" Surprise dripped from that one word. "Why?" It reflected in her eyes as she stared at him. Even the dog looked up as if waiting to hear his explanation.

"Yes, quite true." He nodded. "I have missed having someone around during Christmastide. It was always a time of togetherness with my family. I might enjoy it now if I can, but if you don't wish to—"

"Hush, Thomas." Damn, but he adored the sound of his name in her voice. When was the last time he sat beside a woman to do nothing but talk? It was incredibly… freeing. She laid a hand on his arm, and he nearly vaulted off the bench. "I have already made plans to decorate. It is time to discover who we are together, and perhaps find contentment or at the very least, friendship."

"Indeed." He could do nothing but nod. "I am done with being lost. It is good to start over, I think." Yet, how many times would it take, and what would happen if he cocked this chance up? Destroyed all the chances that followed?

Despite his earlier annoyance at the situation and being forced to wed, he was far too interested to fail now.

Chapter Eight

December 20, 1817

Olivia set down her knitting with a sigh when a handful of people streamed into the room. She was almost finished with yet another baby-sized blanket, and this interruption would delay that lovely moment. However, the arrival of so many people cheered her considerably, for the afternoon was overcast with a steady rain that had brought the chill. Kip sat on a sofa cushion near her position with his nose tucked beneath his tail in slumber.

Then she frowned. Wallace had a footman, a maid, and a modiste in tow. The footman carried a ladder while the maid brought in a box filled to brimming with evergreens and other greenery fit for the holiday season, while the modiste trailed a couple of seamstresses behind her, both with their arms full of gowns and other clothing.

"What is happening, Wallace?" She didn't recall that she'd had appointments today.

"We have secured the greenery you requested, my lady. Already it has gone up in the downstairs parlor and entry hall. Also, Mrs. Forrester has arrived with some of the gowns you ordered." The older man flashed a grin that pulled an answering one from her. "It is quite a busy afternoon."

"So it would appear. Where is the viscount?" Since it was a Saturday, there was no excuse that business would keep him away.

"I believe he had an errand but should return shortly."

"Thank you." She put her knitting aside on the sofa where she'd set up a nest of sorts then stood as another pair of footmen entered the room with a folding silk privacy screen. "What do you need me from me, Mrs. Forrester?"

"To try on the gowns, of course, my lady." The modiste directed the seamstresses to drape the clothing over the backs of every available sofa or chair while she guided the footmen to set up the privacy screen. "And since your Mr. Wallace tells me your time is spoken for this afternoon with the Christmastide decorating, I assumed you would wish to put the gowns on here while supervising."

It hadn't occurred to her that she might need to take care of multiple tasks at the same time. "Oh, all right." When her gaze fell on some of the jewel-colored gowns, a tiny thrill went down her spine. "The gowns are beautiful." Truly, she had never owned pieces made of such luxurious fabrics with such delicate lace trims or expensive threads.

"Well, you *did* provide the fabric. I was merely inspired by them." The woman plucked a gown of dark green satin from one of the sofas. It sparkled with hundreds of tiny clear and silver glass beads on the skirt. "We will begin with this one. I want to make certain the fit is just right in the event you and Lord Ashbury attend an event this holiday season. With your fiery hair, it will look *très magnifique* in the candlelight."

Thomas isn't the socializing type... unless it is at a club or gaming den.

For that matter, she hadn't seen him after they'd strolled in the square yesterday, and because of that, she was learning his habits. Once he shared anything personal or emotional, he retreated either into himself or physically away, as if he feared her reaction or despised himself for the vulnerability. Not that she blamed him. Her whole motivation for years had been to seek him out and make him pay for what he'd done to her best friend, and when she'd discovered she only had part of the story, revenge had no place in it.

What do I do with my time now?

Realizing the modiste awaited an answer, Olivia sighed. "Very well, but I doubt we have engagements or even dinner parties for the upcoming holiday." For that matter, why not? Was Ashbury ashamed of marrying a woman with freckles and Irish roots? Annoyance prickled through her chest. It was something she needed to ask him about.

"Wonderful! One of the footmen took a few boxes to your rooms. Those contain fripperies and unmentionables and underthings."

She nodded. "I appreciate all the work you have put into a whole new wardrobe." With another frown, she took a few steps toward the privacy screen set up at the back of the room away from the windows and the fireplace where blessed warmth emanated from the jaunty fire behind the ornamental grate. "I didn't understand how involved it would be or how much larger such a wardrobe would be from my ordinary one."

"A viscountess is quite an important personage in the *ton*, my lady. People will look to you for inspiration and guidance."

Never had that been pressed upon her more than in this moment. "Quite," she managed in a choked whisper. Since marrying Ashbury, she suddenly had a voice and power within a vast social network. With her help and funding, she could gently use her patronage to various causes as a catalyst for change, further work with the people she already did. Make a difference.

It was heady stuff indeed.

As she moved behind the screen with a seamstress to assist with the clothing, Wallace directed the footmen to begin hanging evergreen swags and other greenery about the room. She rather enjoyed the hustle and bustle throughout the room. It made her think that perhaps, with time, there might be a family to fill the house with echoes of conversation and laughter. For now, she had her new staff and she adored coming to know them better. Already, she'd discovered one of the maids fancied one of the footmen, and she wanted nothing more than to support in matchmaking endeavors.

The cool satin slid over her skin like water. It was lovely, and she reveled in it. Deeper and richer than the hue she'd worn on her wedding day, this gown's bodice was lower, and the short sleeves puffed. Beadwork was sprinkled over the neckline. The full skirt slipped about her feet like a whisper.

"This gown feels wonderful, Mrs. Forrester."

"Come out and let me see it, check the fit."

Olivia stepped from behind the screen and did a little twirl for the modiste. "Well?"

"Hmm." The older woman frowned as she regarded her with a critical eye. "Perhaps it needs a red or silver bow about the waist?"

"That would take away some of its splendor, don't you think?" Then her attention was pulled to a footman who tried to nail evergreen swags over the fireplace. "No, that's too high!" She rushed around the modiste and then made her way to the ladder. "Come down from there. I'll show you where it should be hung."

The footman glanced at Wallace, who shrugged. With nothing for it, he climbed down, still holding the evergreens.

"Lady Ashbury, I really should caution you about climbing in the gown," Mrs. Forrester began as she came toward the fireplace.

"I will be careful. Don't worry." Then, with a handful of fabric clutched lightly in a fist, Olivia darted up the ladder while another footman held it steady. It was a bit risky in her bare feet, but she balanced on the mantel; there was at least a foot of space there, and if she stood flat against the wall, it wasn't so bad. Looking over her shoulder, she addressed the first footman. "John, hand me the first swag so I can demonstrate the height."

He came up the ladder halfway and put the end of the evergreen into her hands. "Be careful, my lady."

"All will be well." It was slightly gratifying to know so many people worried over her wellbeing. The pungent scent of evergreens wafted to her nose as she put it against the wall and its striped paper of light blue and cream. "We want it high enough to be seen over the mantel and candles that will rest here but not so high that potential guests strain their necks." As she spoke, she moved the greenery about on the wall until she found a height that she liked.

"Hellfire and damnation, what is going on in here?"

The ring of the viscount's voice as well as the surprise and confusion therein startled Olivia more than it should have. So much so that she lost her footing, and forgetting she didn't have much space to work with, a squeal of terror left her throat. For a few seconds, she was weightless, clutching onto the evergreen swag as if would keep her from falling.

A few murmurs of dismay sounded in the room, but it was Thomas who rushed across the room just in time to catch her in his arms while the evergreen swag went flying.

"Oh, goodness!" There was nothing quite like being cradled in a man's strong arms. The feel of them beneath her knees and around her back had a flurry of butterflies erupting through her belly. She met his light brown, almost tawny, gaze, and he stared back for the space of a few heartbeats. "Thank you. I rather think it might have hurt if I took a spill to the floor." Had his jaw always been that sharp and the faint dent in his chin that deep?

"No doubt it would have. Whatever possessed you to do something as foolish as to stand on the mantel in your bare feet?" There was an intensity in his eyes that stole away her breath.

"I, uh... Well, I thought to show the footman... I promised to help with the Christmastide decorating, and then the modiste came with gowns to do last fittings on…"

"It seems you thrive on chaos, Lady Ashbury."

Why couldn't she stop staring at his mouth? "It does provide undeniable energy." Her voice was hushed as she slipped her left hand about his nape.

"Indeed." Desire darkened his eyes and lit tiny fires in her blood. Without taking his attention from hers, he ordered everyone from the room. "I require a few moments alone with my wife. All of this can be resumed later in the afternoon."

"There are still fittings, Lord Ashbury—"

"Come back in an hour, madam."

"But, my lord, there are certain things—"

"They can wait, Wallace." His tone brooked no arguments and sent a shiver down her spine. "Close the door on your way out."

"Of course, my lord." Then he gestured for everyone in the room to clear the space. With a last glance filled with speculation at them, the butler closed the door behind him.

As her heartbeat accelerated, Olivia lifted an eyebrow. "What did you wish to speak with me about that brought out the command in your tones?"

"Seeing you on such an unorthodox perch as the mantel—precarious though it was—nearly had my heart attacking me, but it is the gown that has held me captive. In it, you are Christmastide personified, and I am far too aroused with you here in my arms like this."

Need skittered down her spine to lodge into her core. Her breath caught. "What do you intend to do about that?" Perhaps indulging in an interlude would take the edge off the charged tension that had been roiling between them since they'd wed.

"This." Slowly, he released the arm beneath her knees and let her slide down his body until her feet reached the floor, then he cupped her cheek, tilted her head up, and just as slowly claimed her lips.

A tiny sigh escaped before Olivia curled one hand into his lapel and slipped the other hand to his back. There was nothing else to do but kiss him back. The strength of him beneath her fingertips both empowered her and put her in awe of him. That day in the study, she hadn't been as acutely aware of him as she was now.

He moved over her mouth, taking what he wanted, demanding that she give him respect and regard, telling her without words there was a world of wicked promise waiting if she would but give into him.

And in this moment, she had every intention of doing just that. Despite the fact that their marriage had been forced, she had wedded this man of her own free will and they had a life together come what may. As she held this man in an embrace, this man who was broken and hurting as she, she needed the freedom to explore him as she'd wished since that first kiss, to prompt healing by perhaps forgetting everything within the throes of passion.

With a groan, he pulled slightly away, searched out her gaze. "If you continue to look at me like that, we'll both be in trouble."

"As if you didn't come into this room with scandal on your mind." The flutters in her belly increased. "How am I looking at you, then?" Awareness of him rushed over her in a heated tide, but she *knew*. She wanted this man in the basest of ways, wanted to experience that tide of physical bliss only coupling with him would bring.

"As if you wish to do unspeakable things to me." His eyes darkened as his fingers tightened slightly on her arms.

"Mmm, that sounds perfectly lovely, but do *you* wish that as well?" It had been too long since she'd indulged in such a way.

"I am two seconds away from tearing that gown from your body, but it is far too beautiful to damage, and I might wish to introduce you to my friends if you promise to wear it." Thomas put his lips to the shell of her ear. "Unless you don't mind. In which case, I'll have you naked in a thrice."

Olivia snorted. "There is no need to destroy a perfectly good gown, and Mrs. Forrester would not be pleased." Feeling all too saucy, she turned around and offered him her back. "You can undo the laces and we'll go from there."

"Gladly." Seconds later, his fingers were at the laces and his lips at her nape. Both sent shivers twisting up her spine and she fairly shook from anticipation. When the gown gaped, he eased it down her arms and torso, pausing briefly to drag his lips along the column of her throat and brush his thumbs against the underside of her breasts through the lawn of her shift. "Next time, do not think to do something as foolish as balance bodily on a fireplace mantel."

"Why, surely you aren't worried about me, Ashbury," she asked in her best teasing tone while awareness prickled over her skin.

"You are my wife," he said softly into her ear as he pushed the gown from the remainder of her form. "And my responsibility. Neither do I want to see you hurt." His fingers worked the laces of her stays. Seconds later, the garment fell to the floor at her feet. "Knowing you, my life would be rendered miserable if that were to occur."

That took some of the edge off the desire throbbing through her. "Old habits are difficult to break, I'm afraid."

"Indeed." In short order he divested her of the lawn shift, and once she was stark naked, he cupped her breasts, pulling her backside against his front. "However, the distraction you represent is quite intriguing."

Her breath caught when he strummed his fingers over her rapidly tightening nipples. Sensation shivered through her. Olivia wriggled her hips into his and was rewarded by the insistent press of his erection at the small of her back. "I have been called worse." Those were particularly memories she didn't want to remember.

"Those men, the ones who overlooked you due to your freckles, hair, or ancestry were fools, but if they weren't, you and I wouldn't be standing here now." As he nuzzled the crook of her shoulder, he fondled her breasts and worried her nipples.

Oh, how she adored the preliminary caresses that built into frantic need. "While I appreciate those words, you wouldn't have chosen me for your bride either. We were forced to wed, and we have to square with that."

"Bah. Don't muddy this moment." Seconds later, he turned her about in his arms then claimed her mouth in a series of searing kisses that left her far too heated and breathless.

Her head spun, but she wanted him as naked as she. "There are far too many clothes still separating us, Ashbury," she said as she manipulated the buttons of his jacket of bottle green superfine.

"On this I quite agree with you." Never breaking eye contact, he stepped back a few paces. Never had a man made as short work with undressing as the viscount. The second he stood before her without a stitch on, he let her drink his form in with her eyes. The cheeky bastard even watched her with a faint smirk on his face while she unashamedly roved her gaze over his person. "I haven't garnered complaints over the years."

She stopped short of rolling her eyes to the heavens. Men and their egos. "You will do nicely, I think." And once more she ogled him, couldn't wait to shove her fingers through the mat of heavy blond hair covering the upper plains of his chest or follow the thin ribbon of the same down his flat abdomen that ended in a golden nest at the base of an impressively erect shaft.

"Then let us waste no more time." Like when he'd crossed the room to catch her, he moved quickly, encouraging her to sit on one of the sofas not in the same grouping as where Kip still—hopefully—slept next to her knitting. He kneeled before her on the rug, held her head between his large hands, and set out to apparently kiss her senseless.

For that is what it felt like as her head swam and passion clouded her mind. The sandalwood and citrus scent of him infiltrated her nose, made her almost drunk on him, and as he glided his hands over her skin, caressing and teasing as he went, she shuddered from the sheer eroticism of the act. The appreciative gleam in his eyes as he devoured her naked form with his gaze sent chills of anticipation over her skin, and then he gave her another round of adoration as he went exploring with his fingers, tongue, and lips.

Not once did she have the opportunity to do the same on him, for each time she tried, he caught her hands and held her wrists lightly behind her back with one hand.

"Not yet."

"That's not fair." She tried to free her wrists—halfheartedly at that—but it was too delicious feeling slightly restrained by him. It was criminal a man could look like that, and she couldn't take her attention from him.

"Nothing is quite fair when carnal pleasures are at play." His grin was genuine as he lifted his head from one of her breasts to meet her gaze. "Your turn will come… after I send you flying a time or two."

"By then I will have forgotten all about my want to explore," she said in some pique, for she did so need to bring him to shuddering awareness as he was doing to her.

"More's the pity, because I know what I bring to this coupling."

A stab of annoyance lanced through her chest. "Of all the arrogant, self-important—"

With a chuckle, Thomas quelled her outburst with a kiss that nearly made her forget her own name. Then he proceeded to kiss and caress every inch of her body. With each touch and lick and nibble, Olivia's commonsense faded. In its place came heat and pinwheeling pleasure. She freed her wrists but only had the wherewithal to clutch at his shoulders, his upper arms as he teased her without ceasing. His hot mouth on her breasts, his tongue teasing her sensitized nipples, his experienced fingers between her thighs all left her gasping and wriggling with excitement and fairly humming in heightened need.

The last time she'd entered into scandal with a man had been over two years before, and that had ended in disaster as she'd told Ashbury in the square, but she hadn't told him all of that story. Those thoughts danced through her mind now, playing hide and seek with the more lovely thoughts his touches provoked. There was no moving away from the past; it was always there, waiting to strike and cloud the present.

Seeking to banish those more unpleasant thoughts, Olivia tried to tug him upward to join her on the sofa, but he wasn't nearly done with her. "Ashbury, stop being so damned stubborn."

"Ah, there's the temper coming out. I'd wondered where you were hiding it." But the maddening man merely grinned and watched her as he continued to ply the swollen button at her center with varying degrees of friction. "Give in and that anger can be channeled into other, more pleasurable ways."

"Let me touch you, damn you!" Truly, she was slowly losing her mind to be denied that simple gift.

"Soon." He kissed her again and kept on with those talented fingers that strummed over her flesh again and again and *again*.

With a gasp, and a light bite to his bottom lip to show her ire, she pulled away. "I cannot survive much more of your torture."

"That is too bad, for I have much to give you still." Yet he paused, leaving her hovering so very close to the edge of breaking. "I think a different tact is needed to see you fall, hmm, Lady Ashbury?" Before she could try to puzzle out his intent, Thomas rolled one of her nipples and took the other into the hot cavern of his mouth.

The sensations were nearly overwhelming, and she slipped to the edge of the sofa. He kept her from falling completely off that piece of furniture by catching her thighs and spreading her even further open for his perusal. "Christ, but you are gorgeous." His breath steamed her skin seconds before he put his mouth over the center of her heat where his fingers had just teased.

"Oh!" The difference in texture between his fingers and his tongue was pure insanity, and the eddies of pleasure he invoked worked to separate her from reality. It was one of her favorite parts of coital teasing. "Yes, yes. I need more." She fell backward on the sofa, held herself upright on her elbows, and when the viscount followed her hints beautifully, release rushed up to catch her. Before she was ready, Olivia shattered into a million pieces with a half-muffled squeal. "Thomas!"

He ignored her in favor of drawing out her pleasure with his tongue and teeth. When she tugged on his hair as contractions rocked her core, he finally lifted his head. His chuckle further heightened her need, and another wave broke over her.

"We have just begun." With a wicked gleam in his eyes, her husband came back up to kiss her lips.

"Show me what else you can do." She wasted no time in shifting upon the sofa so that she lay upon that piece of furniture while pulling him down over her. "To see if the rumors surrounding your carnal skill are true." As Olivia's heartbeat accelerated, she smoothed her palms over his chest, dragged them along the length of his body. His muscles clenched beneath her touch and still she caressed him, moving lower and lower until she glanced her fingertips over the rampant part of him. Oh, that meant he would be so satisfying once they finally were joined. When he hissed a warning, she chuckled. "I cannot wait to play with this." As she spoke, she curled her fingers about his shaft, which prompted a groan from him.

"Hold." His whispered command rumbled in her chest. "There is time for that later if we should do this again." As he caught her hands, he encouraged her arms up over her head and he fit the wide head of his member to her opening. "I am too well primed."

"Good." Need throbbed hard through her core. "Finish me, then, and make it memorable." A restless feeling coursed through her, made stronger by his delay.

"It will go quickly, for it has been some time," he said, and with a flex of his hips, he entered her in a long, smooth glide. He filled her, stretched her, fitted himself to her like a lost puzzle piece, and he didn't stop until he was fully seated.

"Dear lord. So big." And he felt incredible. A sigh shuddered from her as she wriggled into a more comfortable position. "We shall have another go of it to make certain we savor it." Not wanting to spoil the joining with talking, Olivia canted her hips and took him deeper, and the sensation was so exquisite, another moan escaped.

Thomas didn't answer with words. He held his weight on his forearms as he stroked into her, slowly at first, the thrusts leisurely and tender as if he had all the time in the world. He held her gaze, but she couldn't read the emotions in his eyes. When she looped her arms about the breadth of his shoulders, clinging to him, her legs twined about his waist, he increased his pace. Over and over, he pushed. Harder and harder he moved as if he wished to join them permanently. He worked with such enthusiasm that he scooted them up the sofa's surface.

With each pass, the band of restless need stacking within her grew. Oh, how well she remembered this act, and it was one of the most wonderful things a woman could experience in life. When Thomas' strokes continued, she braced her hands against the arm of the sofa to prevent her head from smacking into it as his thrusting grew ever faster and more urgent, and she met them as best she could.

"More." Did it make her look desperate to enjoy the act so much? Release came upon her far too soon. It roared with veracity through her already primed body with an intensity that stole her breath. "Thomas!" Pleasure crashed over her, pulled her down beneath its waves and she was powerless to resist. She drowned in it, reveled in it, gave herself up to the vortex swirling within. With a shout of pure satisfied joy, she shattered for the second time that afternoon.

"Damn!" Thomas succumbed to his own bliss with a muted roar. At the last second, he removed his length from her body. The warmth of his coming splattered upon her knee and lower leg. It would leave a mess and stain on the upholstery, but in this moment, she couldn't rouse enough strength to worry. Then he collapsed on top of her, his breathing ragged in her ear, the strong bands of his arms around her once more.

As her breathing returned to normal and the residual tremors faded, Olivia snuggled into his embrace. Sated and relaxed, she sighed. "That was indeed worth the drama surrounding our union thus far." Yet he obviously didn't want everything a future entailed with her if he ensured that she wouldn't become pregnant from this encounter.

"Perhaps, but does it change anything?" The inquiry was graveled from the emotion in his voice.

Kip chose that moment to utter a series of yapping barks from his spot on the floor directly in front of the sofa where they lay. *Oh, dear.* How long had he been there, and more to the point, what had he witnessed? Heat flooded her cheeks.

"Damned annoying dog." A moment later, Thomas stirred and rolled off her, collecting his clothing as he walked toward the door. Fleetingly, his gaze met hers, but she couldn't read the emotions there. "I… Don't ask me to apologize for…" He didn't finish the thought before shoving his legs into his breeches and then leaving the room.

Olivia heaved a sigh as she stared at the ceiling and offered a hand to Kip, who licked her fingers. One step forward, twenty back. If Thomas would stop carrying his burden by himself, he could start healing. Perhaps she would have to do that first and show him.

No matter that making herself so vulnerable was terrifying.

CHAPTER NINE

December 21, 1817

THOMAS WAS AT odds with himself, for his world continued to shift around him as if he were tossed about in a storm not of his making. Yesterday, he'd consummated his union with Olivia, had claimed her body in the drawing room like a man possessed, and he still couldn't wrap his head around that experience.

Yet it had changed nothing within the relationship, had meant nothing, or so he'd told himself over and over again since it had happened. It had been naught but an outlet, for they'd both needed the physical release, but when he'd stepped into the drawing room and had seen the bustling activity, watched her as a part of the chaos, stand on the mantel in that green gown, the shift that had begun in his study earlier had continued.

And he'd started the slide down a slippery slope, especially when she'd tumbled off the mantel. He hadn't thought, merely reacted. The second she'd landed in his arms and had locked eyes with him, the dynamic between them had slightly changed and the desire simmering in his blood had boiled over. In that moment, he'd wanted her beyond all reason, and he didn't care what the staff or her modiste thought when he'd ordered everyone out.

He'd only wanted her.

What the hell is wrong with me?

Shouldn't he always remember Cynthia and what had happened to her, the grief that he still struggled with all these years later? A part of his brain kept reminding him she was gone, but Olivia was here in the flesh and quite vibrant, and they were married. It was a logical conclusion, and life was certainly for the living, but his heart kept offering a protest.

"Argh!" His utterance startled a maid that he passed in the corridor.

Why the devil was his mind in such confusion? Shouldn't he be able to view the matter in shades of black and white? He could give his body to his wife but keep his heart back for the woman he'd fallen hard for years ago? The woman who would have been his viscountess and the mother of his children?

In a brown study, he paused near the staircase to reorder his thoughts, the need to break his fast temporarily thwarted. The simple fact remained that he could no longer ignore Olivia; she kept their circumstances front and center, wouldn't let him hide. For that she had his respect, and damn it all, the more he thought about her, the greater the awareness of her grew. They had been wed for four days, and already her presence had seeped into his house, for she had quietly brought order where there was low-grade chaos before.

How had she done it? And for that matter, how had he missed the signs? Already, the staff appeared happier and more content. Had he done such a slip-shod job of it on his own, then?

Of course I have. What I've been doing hasn't been living. I have woven a prison of sorts around me—around them—because I've been too damned comfortable being miserable.

Except, after the initial anger and horrid attitude directly following the nuptial ceremony, somehow being in Olivia's company had taken the edge off that misery. He'd missed the closeness associated with having a woman in his life, missed that camaraderie, that chumminess, and no matter what his heart told him, he wanted to know more about the woman he'd taken to wife, longed to hear her stories and understand why there was pain deep in the depths of her eyes when she didn't think anyone was looking. Would she enjoy it if he read poetry to her, discussed the issues of the day that faced the country?

Perhaps he should work at finding out if only to linger in her company, and the house did look rather homey festooned with evergreen boughs and fir branches with ribbons, and tin bells, and glass balls tucked amidst the greenery.

"Kip!" The call, laced with annoyance, sliced into his musings, and yanked him back into the present. "Drat you frustrating dog. Come back here at once!"

Quickly, Thomas descended the stairs to the second level. "Olivia? Is all well?" The closer he came to the morning room, the more a string of excited barking filled the air. Followed by the click of canine claws on the floor. Then the dog burst into the corridor from the servants' staircase, no less with his tongue hanging out, his ears and tail perked up, and it looked as if he were grinning and quite amused at being so naughty.

His wife came out of the drawing room, clearly frazzled, but lovely in a day dress of navy wool with pearl buttons down the front. A knitted shawl of thin ivory wool had been thrown about her shoulders. Had she made it herself? Then his attention jogged to her fiery hair, which had been braided and then wrapped into a bun at the back of her head. What he wouldn't give to see those tresses down and free again, to bury his hands in the mass, slowly tilt back her head so he could drink his fill of her lips.

Now is not the time for such thoughts, old boy.

When the dog reached Thomas' location, he pawed at his boots and yapped as if he was all too happy to see him. "Why are you tearing like mad through my house?" Slightly amused but worried about what had precipitated the flight, he picked the dog up and once more tucked him beneath his arm just as Olivia joined them.

"I apologize for him being a nuisance," she said in a breathless voice. "The modiste had come back since she was interrupted yesterday." A blush raged in her cheeks. "I didn't want Kip pawing at them—"

"The gowns or the modiste and her assistant?" he couldn't help but ask merely to tease.

Amusement danced in her eyes. "The gowns, so I turned him out of the room, and I suppose he wandered."

"Think nothing of it." He hadn't seen her since their wild coupling from yesterday, but with her standing so close, the faint scent of lilacs teasing his nose, and the blush on her cheeks that called attention to the sprinkling of golden-brown freckles on those cheeks, the bridge of her nose, her forehead, and knowing he'd seen them all over her body when she'd been naked, his pulse accelerated into a rapid tattoo. "I fear our boy Kip takes too much after me—he doesn't enjoy being left out or ignored."

Was that too much of a revelation into him as a man?

"Ah." Olivia offered him a smile that had his gut and his groin both tightening. "Then that is further proof I named him correctly."

Just now realizing what a lovely sense of humor she had, Thomas' lips twitched. "What are your plans for the day?" The longcase clock at the end of the corridor chimed half-past ten.

"Since I am ravenous, I thought to indulge in breakfast. Having the modiste in so early distracted me from that plan." When she reached for the dog, Thomas held the fluffy rat away. His little legs flailed, and he barked with excitement to have all eyes on him. "If you wish for company and you haven't eaten either, I'll join you."

"I would enjoy that." And it was the first whole truth he'd told her since they'd wed. He offered a grin of his own. "In the meanwhile, what should we do about this rogue?" As they strolled into the morning room, he patted Kip's head.

"You'll behave, won't you?" she said to the dog, came close, and then dropped a kiss to the top of his doggy head. "Just put him beneath the table."

"Very well." Thomas did so as soon as they were seated at the round table. He nodded to the footman, who bustled over with teacups and a teapot. "Is the new wardrobe to your liking?" Part of him was glad she'd made immediate inroads into outfitting herself as his viscountess while another part resented the expenditure, even if it had been forced into the marriage contracts.

"It's wonderful and so pretty." When she offered a smile, the world seemed to spin about him. "Thank you for its purchase. My brother was rather stingy with his purse strings, but at least he let me choose my own fabrics from what he had in his warehouses."

"If the gowns are in the same vein as what I saw yesterday, I would say you have an eye for textures and colors." Bah! Was he actually flirting with his wife?

"Thank you. Some of the gowns are cut rather more scandalously than others, but some of the underthings are of the finest lawn and have the prettiest embroidery." Despite the animation in her face and the excitement in her voice, she colored again and shook her head. "My apologies for rambling. I adore lovely clothing and how it makes me feel."

Those same things he took for granted being born into privilege, and what was more, he took pleasure in giving her that delight. "I imagine your parents would be proud of the woman you've become." As he spoke, he stroked a hand over Kip's head and scratched behind his ears. The canine was still ridiculous, but there was something about petting him that soothed a bit of Thomas' ire.

"Oh, I can only hope. Papa was a very opinionated man who talked often of Ireland and the hardships going on there. He'd hoped I would meet and marry a man with a title connected to his home country, said I could do much for my people if that occurred."

"But that wasn't your dream."

"No, it wasn't." She nodded her thanks when the footman put a plate loaded with breakfast foods in front of her. "It still isn't."

Knots tightened in his gut. "You regret marrying me?" he asked in a barely audible voice. Suddenly his appetite had fled, and he frowned at his own plate.

"The first two days, I did, but then I hated you at the time."

"And now?" He could hardly breathe, and as he watched her face, he slipped the dog a bit of ham steak beneath the table.

"And now, I have changed my mind on both counts." That beguiling smile returned when she glanced at him from over the rim of her teacup.

"Oh?"

Olivia nodded, but she didn't expand on the topic.

By increments, he relaxed. "So then I don't need to expect to have the tip of your blade pressed against my neck any time soon?"

"Perhaps not." Another blush splashed over her cheeks. She squealed when Kip jumped into the chair beside her and then hopped onto the tabletop. "Kip!" But the dog didn't heed the exclamation. He darted over to her plate, snagged her ham steak with his pointy teeth, and then returned to the floor the same way he'd come. The click of his claws as he beat a hasty retreat out of the room left them both stunned. "Oh, that dog!" Using her linen napkin, she cleaned up a trail of butter and scattered scrambled eggs left behind by the canine thief.

"His manners do need work." Thomas couldn't help but chuckle at the look of bafflement on her face. "Here." Quickly, he cut off a bite-sized piece of his ham steak, speared it with his fork, and then brought it to her lips. "Eat. We will lecture the dog later."

"He has gone renegade since we moved in."

"Perhaps he is out of sorts now that there's a new male in your life."

"How interesting." She held his gaze as she opened her mouth, and he slipped the tidbit in. When her lips closed briefly over his fork, he stared at them. Damn, but he wanted a kiss. After she swallowed, he took back his utensil. "Thank you."

"You're welcome." He gestured to the footman. "The lady needs a new plate."

"Of course, my lord." While the younger man busied himself with exchanging the dishes, Thomas sipped his tea.

Once the footman had everything squared away, Thomas dismissed him. "Thank you for joining me this morning. After yesterday, I wasn't certain where we stood."

Not that he was sure now, but sitting here beside her was... lovely. Obviously, he and Cynthia weren't afforded time for that, since the bulk of their relationship had to be conducted in secret, but since time had passed, he had come to see a union between them probably wouldn't have worked. He hadn't truly known the woman she was, for they hadn't talked of anything beyond the heat between them and the perhaps puppy-like adoration.

Well, damn. I've been a fool. That truth didn't discount his feelings or lessen them.

"We are... taking each day as it comes." An enigmatic light lit the depths of her gray eyes. "We will meet those unique challenges, but we'll do it together, and isn't that more than we had before?"

"Yes, of course." He pushed the scrambled eggs around his plate with the tines of his fork. "I rather like this." Then he cleared his throat, for he didn't want to appear weak in front of her. "Without the dog's thievery, that is."

She chuckled. "True." Cutting into her new ham steak, she asked, "Tell me how your caricature drawing came about. I wasn't lying when I told you those sketches were quite good. You could be an artist of some acclaim if you'd let yourself."

"Ha." Imagine the scandal if the truth came out. "I began drawing a few years ago. I happened to be cooling my heels, waiting for Pennington to wrap up a conversation with someone after the Lords ended one night, and happened to overhear one of the other men making jest of the plight of a tenant on his estate. It enraged me, for that type of derogatory assumptions was how my father thought, and I wanted to part of it."

"So you set out to make jest of those kinds of men right back."

Thomas shrugged. "A bit, but once I developed a knack and talent for the drawings, I started to sell the political cartoons to some of London's most popular newspapers."

"Secretly, of course," she added with a wink.

"Of course." Knowing he needed to eat, he ate a few forkfuls and washed the food down with the remainder of his tea. "And I did it because I didn't feel my voice was being heard in the Lords." Truth be known, it was more than that. "I continued the drawings in the hopes I could make my point in a different way, get more people than my peers thinking. If I can make the lords as well as the populace change their views to help the good of the nation, then I have done something correctly. Things *must* change, and soon in England." Because it wasn't fair to give good fortune to one class over the others. Cynthia had helped him to see that. "Over the years it became an outlet for my lingering feelings, but it hasn't proven enough to help."

For long moments, Olivia peered at him. Finally, she nodded. "I understand the need to keep busy. My father died with his brother on a ship with some of their imports. After my mother perished, he threw himself into the business. It was yet another unexpected death where there was no warning given."

"I didn't know. You have my sympathies."

"Thank you." She nodded. "Oh, Thomas, I grow so weary of being taken by surprise when someone leaves. I live in fear that something will happen to my brother, and I'll be left alone."

"Not quite alone. I'm here." Did she not consider him important enough?

"Yes, you are, and I hadn't realized how much I appreciate that in the short time we've been together."

"Does that mean you're thawing toward me?" When she didn't answer, he sighed. "How do you manage to keep your fears at bay?"

"I took up knitting." She said it with a grin that had tiny fires licking through his blood.

"Knitting is, I thought, for the lower classes." He couldn't recall anyone he'd known enjoying such a hobby.

"Why though?" The return of her fiery spirit had desire twisting through his gut. "It is relaxing, and I make beautiful things from it. Additionally, purchasing spun wool and dyes from tenant farmers gives them a much-needed income."

"I hadn't thought to see it in that way." It impressed the hell out of him. She would do great things for his title and hers, and he couldn't be more proud. "What do you make?"

The blush returned to pinken her cheeks. "Blankets, right now. Small enough for babies."

"Oh?" That was a surprise. "What do you do with them?"

Remarkably, tears pooled in her eyes, and she glanced away. "It is a matter dear to my heart but involves even more loss."

Her reference to babies and loss was like the stab of a hot poker to his chest. "And you don't wish to talk about them," he finished in a soft voice. Even though her grief rubbed against his own, he wanted to help her through it.

"I do not." Surreptitiously, she wiped at an escaped tear on her cheek.

"Understandable." Perhaps it was time to share another secret with her even if it meant laying bare his soul as well as his fears. "Join me for an outing around one o'clock today?"

"Why?"

"It is time to talk of my history with you, and perhaps help you in return."

"Oh." She frowned at him with speculation in her eyes. "Is all well?"

"Not at all." Pushing away his plate, he shook his head. "But I want you to know everything. No more secrets or trying to keep a wall between us. We cannot decide a future without the truth given." Surely, he was a nodcock as she peered at him with round eyes, for he wanted to make her proud, and he suspected he couldn't do that if he were stuck in the past. "If you'll excuse me?"

As emotions filled his chest and clogged his throat, he left the room rather more quickly than he should. She would either understand him better or detest him more.

The only consolation was she couldn't hate him any more than he did himself.

CHAPTER TEN

AT THE APPOINTED time, Olivia was ushered into a closed carriage and then closeted inside with her husband. All he'd told her was their destination was Hyde Park. After that, he sat morosely on the bench across from her, staring out the window and disinclined to talk.

All of it had only made her that more curious about him. At breakfast, he'd not spoken of what had occurred between them yesterday in the drawing room. Neither had she mentioned it, for the discussion they had enjoyed had skittered into far too personal territory she hadn't been ready to delve into with him.

But it was a comfortable silence, and the sun shining in through the windows of the vehicle gave a bit of cheer to the otherwise chilly December afternoon. Besides, the silence gave her the opportunity to study her husband as she held Kip in her lap. He served much like a fur-lined muff in that regard.

There was no getting around the fact the viscount was handsome. His blond hair was prone to curl at his collar, for it was slightly longer than current fashion, but it was set in a popular style that spoke of his valet's skill. When he had cause to grin, that gesture revealed a slightly crooked tooth on his bottom jaw which made him approachable, but the slight dimple in his chin gave him an endearing air that played havoc with her heart.

He sat there, seemingly in a relaxed state with an ankle resting on a knee and the folds of his greatcoat falling elegantly about him. Of course he was dressed to impress, and she particularly liked the jacket of sapphire superfine that stretched across the breadth of his shoulders beneath the greatcoat as well as his waistcoat of silver satin sprinkled with embroidered white snowflakes. It seemed a rather jaunty concession to the holiday, a date on the calendar he didn't talk about.

As she roved her gaze over his form and his scent filled the compartment, her mind went to that coupling from yesterday. It had been so unexpected yet so satisfying, for desire had gotten the better of them both. Too quick for her to explore his body as she might have liked, but she felt certain she could tease him into another tryst. A soft smile curved her lips. Yes, she had enjoyed that session with him, perhaps more than she should, especially since today marked a mere five days since they'd been forced to wed.

All that aside, it was a lovely development that they were compatible physically. If only that same enthusiasm would bleed through the rest of their joined lives.

Still, she wanted to hear his voice, needed that, so she wouldn't feel so alone in this moment, for there was something quite forlorn about her husband's demeanor.

"Thomas?"

"Hmm?" He flicked his gaze to her, the brandy depths haunted.

Kip lifted his head and uttered a low bark. For whatever reason, he felt an affinity with the viscount.

"If you could go back and live your life over again—with the knowledge that you have now—would you do it? Would you wish to live those years without making the mistakes you did?"

For the space of far too many heartbeats, he regarded her with stony silence and a stonier expression. Then, he gave her a terse shade of the head. "No." Emotion graveled his voice. "Despite the pain and loss and grief, I had love." One corner of his mouth tilted upward but he didn't give into a full grin. "If I lived my life all over again, I might not experience that, for I might wish to mitigate the losses, and frankly, I would rather have love."

Surprise shivered through her insides. His words were quite romantic. He showed growth even in the small time they had been married. "Love is quite powerful and very elusive. If we are fortunate to find it, we should fight to hold onto it for as long as we can." She blew out a breath. "In the event you wondered, I wouldn't go back either or do anything over again, but with one exception."

"Which is?"

Olivia loosed a sigh. Now was not the time. "I will tell you later." She held Kip a tad too close, for he yelped and then hopped to the floor from her lap, causing her to wrap his leather lead about her hand a few times.

He frowned. "Fair enough, but sooner or later, we will both need to strip down our souls, stand before each other in that vulnerability with nothing else to hide behind to discover if we are strong enough to survive what we have been given."

"I know." She couldn't help but nod. When had he become so wise or willing to come out of the shadows himself? Did he want the future a marriage entailed? Want all of it?

And more to the point, did she? It was well and good spending his coin and buying clothing or fripperies, or enjoying a quick carnal tryst with him, but it was quite another promising him a lifetime, come what may.

What of the dreams she'd had prior to becoming a viscountess?

In short order, the carriage rumbled into the park. The driver let them out at the main gate. From there, they strolled toward the Serpentine despite the chill. Sunlight sparkled off the water like tiny diamonds. Soon enough, parts of the river would freeze. As they walked, Kip barked at fallen leaves as well as grass blades then seconds later, he was frightened by a pair of brown geese who'd dared to paddle close to where he investigated the bank. Throughout it all, Thomas remained silent as if he warred with himself over what he would say, but he'd offered her his arm, and though the muscles were tense beneath her fingertips, she clung to his crooked elbow and found it rather nice to stroll beside a man.

My husband. He might be many things, but he didn't beat her, didn't verbally abuse her, didn't take what she hadn't offered, and most certainly hadn't sent her to his estate in the country alone. If he was a bit more morose and maudlin than she'd anticipated, the same might be said of her.

Well-matched indeed, if they could move past this bump.

"Where are we going?"

"Not far." A breath of frustration escaped him. "If you are curious, this is where I go every other day if the weather is fair."

"Ah." Would he finally trust her with that information? She didn't want to show too much anticipation for fear he would change his mind. Kip pulled at the lead and temporarily separated her hand from Thomas' arm. When she came back to him, a muscle ticced in his cheek. Was he angry with her, the dog, or the situation?

"I have always adored Hyde Park," he said into the silence as they followed the river past a few families who were also strolling in the sunshine. Seeing everyone bundled up against the chill in the air, some with fur muffs and fur-lined hoods put her in mind of Christmastide. "My governess used to bring me here when I was a young boy. I sailed my first paper boat on the Serpentine." The sound of his chuckle reverberated in her chest. "When I went away to school, I often daydreamed about coming back and exploring through the park. I often did whenever my family was in London." He cleared his throat. "I... There were days when I wished I could have shown my brother the wonders of the Serpentine. He would have been so amazed."

"You have a brother?" How interesting.

"I did. He died many years ago."

"I see. Was he ill?"

"No. He was, ah, born with something not quite right with his brain, which rendered him slower than other children, not quite able to master the simplest of equations or read or even completely dress himself."

"And because of that, your parents sent him away." No wonder Thomas had rebelled against his father's dictates. "Did you see your brother after that?"

"I did not. My father was quite adamant about it. Not long afterward, my mother died. My father and I drifted apart. I spent more and more time in the country."

"Where you met Cynthia and were much in need of a distraction." As stories went, it wasn't remarkable, and it probably happened more often than not in titled families. The *ton* valued perfection and strong bloodlines more than anything else. The Prestwicks couldn't have a damaged son around as a constant reminder of their failure.

"When put so succinctly, it sounds rather dull and horrifying."

"Everyone's story does."

The trill of a child's laughter cut straight through Olivia's heart. With a gasp, she couldn't help but remember the worst day of her life. Tears prickled the backs of her eyelids, and she quickly blinked them away lest Thomas see. Focusing on a pair of black swans that paddled their way toward shore, she smiled at a girl with blonde hair wearing a bright red cloak. As they passed, it was obvious that mental faculties weren't all present with her slack expression and slightly bulging eyes, but she was a joyful little thing, laughing as she tossed torn pieces of bread into the water for the swans.

"Come." He followed her line of vision, and he swallowed hard. "Just there." The viscount led her to a small grouping of evergreen trees. A fallen log sat nearby. When he urged her over, he patiently waited until she'd seated herself before he did the same. His sleeve brushed hers, and heated tingles trembled to her elbow.

Instead of immediately following into conversation, another round of silence brewed between them. Kip tugged anxiously at his lead. She leaned down, tried to calm his nerves with a pet to his head.

Eventually, she grew restless as well. "Why are we here?"

"God, this is going to be difficult," he whispered, not to her but almost to himself. Thomas kept his focus across the Serpentine, the narrowest section where the girl in the red cloak fed the swans. A few other adults stood in her vicinity, people Olivia presumed were her parents and a governess, for they looked on with smiles and encouraging nods. Clearly, the little girl was the light of their world.

"Breathe in, breathe out, Ashbury." Since no one was immediately around them, she dared to lay a gloved hand on his thigh. He flinched as if he'd been punched, but then relaxed by increments. "Start at the beginning."

A huff escaped him. "Well, I have already told you the beginning. When I fell in love with Cynthia."

"Oh." Her chest tightened, for she hadn't thought they'd talk again so soon about her.

"Over the course of knowing you, I realize what I thought was a deep, abiding love for Cynthia was naught but intense attraction and affection. Much like what Kip has for me." He glanced at the dog, who pawed at his boot before trotting back to run beneath the hem of her skirting. "Perhaps it was reckless, but when one is in the grip of such high emotion and the woman in question says she loves you back, one tends to separate a bit from reality."

"Love is love, Thomas. It matters not what you think it was in hindsight, for at that point you are far removed from it."

"Perhaps." The word was a barely audible whisper. "In any event, what I told you was only part of the story. Cynthia and I loved each other. I was blinded by that feeling, the way I didn't feel as worthless or lost when I was with her, encouraged her into my company more and more. Perhaps it was a way to make my father notice me, or a way to forget about the more difficult parts of my life, but I threw everything that I was into that relationship." He stared out at the Serpentine with his forearms resting on his knees and his gloved hands dangling between. "Regardless, I fell hard, and she came right along with me."

Olivia nodded. "I wish she would have trusted me with that information. I would have been so happy for her." There was no denying the viscount had a certain charm about him, enough that people fell beneath his spell when he truly applied himself.

"Wouldn't that have been something?" He snorted as if it was the funniest joke he'd heard in a month. "Me meeting you, sharing my plans of wedding Cynthia in secret with you, the woman I'm now married to."

"But in that scenario, you and I would never have been forced to wed." There was something a bit sad about that if fate had played out differently.

"True." For long moments he watched the little girl. Her laughter echoed over the water and the swans came out of the water to bedevil her for more bread with their long necks twining about. "As such things go, Cynthia soon told me she was increasing, so plans had to be made." His voice thickened with emotion, and still he wouldn't look at her. "At first, I was terrified of what that might mean for my future. It was such a scandal."

"I find it difficult to believe you were a stranger to such things even at eight and twenty."

"Ha!" For a second, he laughed and even gave her a tight smile before training his gaze back on the little girl. "Those were all minor compared to this. I told you that I lost Cynthia to complications following childbirth."

"Yes." She untangled the lead from her ankles, but Kip was far too restless and refused to settle. "Tell me whatever it is you are dancing about. Release your stranglehold of it, so you don't keep worrying about it."

"When I discovered that my father had sent the baby away, I was livid, but I could hardly raise up a child—and a babe that had obvious mental challenges ahead of it—by myself. Especially a child born from a liaison with a maid, but the midwife told me to which orphanage the girl was sent."

Olivia gasped. "You rescued her." It wasn't a question.

"I did." He nodded and found her gaze with his. The light of triumph shone in his eyes. "I couldn't stand idly by and leave her to fate, so I scoured Town for a worthy couple that might wish for a child that would need care and love far more than the usual babe, and I paid them handsomely to take the girl on. Even paid for a governess who watches over her when the parents aren't available." When she stared, he shrugged. "Her name is Sally—I had the naming of her—and she is right over there." He gestured across the Serpentine to the blonde girl. "She is perfect, at least for her parents. Just look at how they adore her."

Again, Olivia fought off tears. "They certainly get on well together." The girl giggled. She jumped up and down and threw herself multiple times into one of the adults' arms. "However, I don't believe they are the only ones who adore her."

The first crack in his armor occurred when his mask of bravery slipped. Immense sadness lined his face; grief shadowed his eyes as moisture gathered there. "I would have tried to be the most remarkable father I could have been," he admitted in a graveled whisper.

She squeezed her fingers on his thigh as tears fell to her cheeks. "There is no doubt you would have. I've seen how you are with Kip." When her attempt at a joke didn't go over well, she sighed. "You come here to watch her, don't you?"

"I do. Somehow, it makes me feel better to see my daughter is thriving and happy." His voice broke and he fought against his emotions. "It's my wish that she lives her life—however long she has—in happiness and that she knows she is loved. In this, my thoughts are much different than my parents', and because of Sally, I am ashamed I didn't fight harder to see my brother or have him brought home. He must have been so frightened." Tears slipped to his cheeks. "For that I'll never forgive myself."

"You were young, and that wasn't your responsibility." While Kip continued to twine himself about her ankles, she took one of Thomas' hands in hers. "Even if you had protested, your father would have countermanded it. He was the viscount and your father." She couldn't help her tears, and when she sniffled, he pressed his handkerchief into her hand.

"Perhaps, but it wasn't surprising. I also had an uncle who exhibited stunted mental faculties, but he wasn't as bad as my brother or perhaps even Sally." He drew in a shuddering breath and let it ease out. "Any children I might have in the future might be like that." His swallow was audible. "Such children can—and do—die earlier in life than others, and that is both terrifying and saddening. How could I survive that over and over?"

It was certainly a shock, and would take some time to think through since it conflicted with one of the dreams of her heart. No wonder he'd pulled out yesterday instead of releasing his seed into her. For that he had her respect. They would need to talk about every possibility and outcome before going forward. "You wouldn't love any of those children less, though, for whatever time they have. That is what makes you different from most." Now she understood why he was so passionate about changing laws and making a better future for everyone within England. A little piece of her heart went into his keeping. "Never stop following that light, Thomas."

"At times it is just too much." He pressed his fingers to his closed eyes and sat in silence beside her on that fallen tree. Kip, ever attuned to the mood of the people around him, stopped playing with her hem and went over to Thomas, put a paw on his boot toe and whined. "Thank you, Sir Kippington. I never thought a furry rat would have a calming effect on me." So saying, he bent and retrieved the dog, took him into his lap and tucked his greatcoat around him.

Another piece of her heart went over to her husband. "I'm sorry." She patted his thigh. "Cynthia would have been proud, I think." Now she understood why her friend had gone tip over tail for the man. He was kind and compassionate, truly cared about the people who were less fortunate. When a person's heart was that large, it also had more of a capacity for breaking. And she also understood why he seemingly carried the weight of the world on his shoulders. It left her both humbled and pleased. "I am too."

Chapter Eleven

Oh, God.

Now that he'd started talking, the dam he'd kept in place, the lid he'd held over his emotions for too many years had been knocked off, and he wanted to continue telling her of his life and experiences.

"Will you ever meet your daughter in person?" She hadn't removed her hand from his thigh. Awareness battled with comfort from that touch.

"No." He appreciated the fact Olivia hadn't given into histrionics over the revelation or the worries over possible children in their future, and more to the point, she hadn't been disgusted by his admission, but the inquiry hit him in the gut like a sucker punch. "That wouldn't be fair to her or her parents." *Or to me.* "She is happy and content. I don't wish to muck about in her life or make her confused."

A sniffle was the only sound she made that betrayed her reaction to the story. "Would you ever demand her adoptive parents tell her of her real history or lineage?"

"Absolutely not. She doesn't need that sort of anxiety or worry in her life. When I had her placed with that family—I'd heard of them from a friend of a friend of my tailor—I knew that I would never mean anything to her, there would not be any contact between any of the parties, nor would the girl ever know who her real father is." Words stuck in his throat as an ache lodged in his heart. "It is simpler this way for everyone. She is part of my past."

"Yet here you are a few times a week," his wife reminded him in a soft voice. "Torturing yourself by watching her, hoping that somehow you will find redemption, an absolution from the guilt of Cynthia's death."

"Yes." The answer felt yanked from him, but how could Olivia know what he felt deep down in a part of him he had never shown anyone? "Frankly, I don't know if that is possible." When she didn't answer, merely sat beside him in silence, he stroked Kip's head, held onto the dog as if he'd suddenly become the only lifeline. "I was devastated to learn of Sally's likeness to my brother. I remembered how my parents had sent him away, never talked of him, how we were expected to carry on in our lives as if he'd never existed. I rarely saw him, and I knew that I didn't want that sort of existence for my daughter."

"That must have been difficult for you, knowing you'd sired a child but couldn't take care of her in the eyes of a society that judges every little thing."

"It was." Moisture welled in his eyes, and he didn't care if it made him weak in her estimation. He'd not given himself permission to feel all the emotions from that time, but now he was here, and they were flooding through his being with nothing to stop them. "I argued with my father about his decision; I'd wanted that part of Cynthia with me always, but he was adamant. Propriety would be observed at all times. He wouldn't have another son to shame him. The title and appearances meant everything to him." As tears fell to wet his cheeks, Thomas impatiently wiped them away. "I understand that now, but back then, I hated him for it."

Olivia slipped her hand up to clutch his. She threaded their gloved fingers together, and he drew from that support. "You did right by your daughter regardless," she said softly. Her breath clouded around her head from the cold. "Sally looks to be quite happy with that family. Without your interference, her fate could have been much worse." With another sniffle, she dabbled her eyes with his handkerchief.

"I like to hope so. I have made arrangements to take care of her financially for as long as she lives."

"I admire you for that. Most men would have merely walked away, grateful there would be no scandal or repercussions from a forbidden romance." She peered into his face. If she saw the tears, she didn't say anything. "Were you able to hold her before she was taken away? Did you tell her she was loved?" Her voice broke on the last word.

"I did not." For the next few moments, he watched Sally as she and her family finished feeding the swans. The birds went back into the water. One of them trumpeted, and the trill of Sally's laughter echoed through the area. More tears welled in his eyes. "My first concern was for Cynthia. Everything happened so quickly... By the time I came up for air, surrounded by grief and heartbreak, the babe had been taken away. I..." He stifled a sob. "I have never forgiven myself since."

"It wasn't your fault, Thomas. None of it was." She squeezed his fingers. "Well, trysting with Cynthia *was* your fault, but you know what I mean."

While he appreciated her attempt at humor, he shook his head. "I should have fought for her, to have her with me."

"Yes, you should have, but it doesn't matter now." With a sigh, Olivia glanced at Kip, who'd poked his head out of Thomas' greatcoat. "Sally is happy in the life she has. Will *you* ever tell her the truth?"

He shook his head. "I promised long ago I wouldn't disturb her. She doesn't need to know she wasn't wanted or that she was a mistake to cover up, to deny." The struggle to keep more tears at bay proved too much, so he let them fall. Emotions crowded his chest, clogged his throat. "I will forever carry that failing in my heart."

Olivia made a sound of sympathy, but didn't release her hold on his hand. "I feel for you and what you went through, but I'm furious with you for giving the child up."

"Why?" He frowned. Truly, he couldn't understand women at times.

"There are far too many women in London who haven't had your good fortune."

What the devil did that mean? "In social position and wealth?"

"No, you lout." She released his hand, and he mourned the loss of that warmth. When she turned toward him, found his gaze with her hers, anger and sadness mixed in her expression. "I once held a babe in my arms, had that glimmer of a tiny dream, but it wasn't to be. The fact that you have a child you willingly gave up..." The delicate tendons in her throat worked with a hard swallow.

Taking the handkerchief from her, he blotted the moisture from his cheeks. "Why?" Did she have another secret she hadn't revealed?

"I suppose I owe you the remainder of the truth since you told me yours." She shivered beside him but resisted his attempt to take her hand. "My last affair ended abruptly only because I discovered that I was increasing." There was so much sorrow in her tone, it made his heart squeeze. "It was the height of scandal, of course, and would have meant I needed to leave London in high disgrace. It would have demanded my life become reordered, but I didn't care."

"Did you tell your lover?"

"Yes, of course, which precipitated his ending of the relationship." Her eyes were luminous with tears, the gray depths clouded with grief. "I retired to my brother's country estate anyway, for I was all too thrilled to prepare for a baby." She trained her attention on Sally and her family as they departed. "But that was all for naught. The babe was stillborn. I held him in my arms afterward, but he had already expired."

His chest ached as if he'd been punched. How she'd managed to carry on with that secret without outwardly breaking, he had no idea, but his respect for her soared. "I am so sorry."

She nodded. A sob wrenched from her throat. "How I wanted that child, Thomas! He would have been my very own family. He would have been someone who could have loved me unconditionally, who I could have loved, who might have filled the hole in my heart after losing nearly everyone in my life." Emotion mottled her face, made her gray eyes darkened to charcoal. "Instead, I was left with empty arms and far too much heartache and grief than one woman should have." For a few moments, she dissolved into tears.

The sight of her upset tugged at his heart. "I'm glad you told me. No one should carry such a burden alone." Thomas pressed his handkerchief into her hand, felt ineffectual in the face of her sorrow, so he slipped an arm about her shoulders and encouraged her head onto his shoulder despite them being in public.

She cried for a few minutes before she quieted. "Thank you for listening." A shuddering sigh left her throat. "I would have adored that life, hidden away at my brother's cottage with a child. A simple, happy life."

"Knowing that scandal had ended your previous existence?" He brushed his hand up and down her arm.

"Of course." Olivia shrugged. "I would have had a child. Been exquisitely happy, for it has long been a dream of mine. I would have had my arms filled whereas now they aren't."

Yet I don't know if I can fulfill that dream for you. Did he dare try and see her enceinte even if it meant they could very well have a child who would be like Sally, like his brother? A child with an uncertain future? "Unless it's with Kip?" he asked softly and hoped she might smile, for they both needed a bit of lightness inside of the heaviness they'd shared.

"There is that. While I adore Kip and he filled a void for me, keeping a dog is not the same as having a baby." Her smile was a watery affair, but she patted the dog on his head. "That would have been so powerful, and now... there is nothing. Those hopes are gone."

His throat constricted at the same time his heart squeezed. "And you are trapped in a marriage you never wanted." Would the better part of valor be to let her go? Despite his worries and fears, an image danced into his mind's eye. She was a mother with four stairstep children gathered around her in a country meadow, and they all resembled him in some way. There was a smile curving her lips and a faraway look in her eye that made him strain to see what or whom she gazed at.

Was it him? Dear God, did he want that dream? How had his thinking changed so drastically from a mere five days ago so quickly?

She lifted her head off his shoulder and once more met his gaze. "I don't feel trapped. Not any longer."

"Oh?" Despite the ache in his chest, his heart thumped into a new rhythm as if he hadn't truly been living before.

"There is something between us that warrants nurturing." When she sighed, the warmth of her breath skated across his chin. "I realize that nothing will fill the holes in my heart, and perhaps that responsibility shouldn't be put on anyone, but sharing grief might help me make room for that grief and move around it." Her eyes sparkled with the remnants of tears. "If you will walk that path with me?"

Another wad of emotion crowded his throat. As best he could, he swallowed past it. "It is better than dying alone or being forgotten." That was one of his greatest fears. Without having answers, Thomas ushered her into his arms despite the potential scandal. He didn't care; she was his wife and she needed comforting. "I am sorry life has been disappointing."

She rested a hand on his chest. "For you as well."

Damn, but his heart ached, for both what he'd lost in the past and what he might forfeit in the future if he didn't change. Resting his cheek against her bonnet, he shed more tears in an effort to cleanse himself of things he'd stubbornly held onto. He hoped Olivia wouldn't judge him for the weakness, yet it didn't feel like a failing as they shared grief together. "Fate hasn't been kind for a while. I have grown used to the disappointment."

"You shouldn't need to, but I understand that all too well." She sniffled and then wiped her nose. "We shall muddle through life knowing we aren't alone. Isn't that better than what we have done before?"

"Indeed. There are worse things." Suddenly, he was glad she was in his life. "Oh, I have something for you."

"You have already given me so much already." But she pulled slightly out of his hold to seek out his gaze again. "What prompted this?"

He shrugged. "I felt it was time, and I want to show you that our union wasn't a mistake." After reaching into a pocket of his greatcoat, he brought out a flat, square-shaped linen-covered jewelry box which he offered to her with a flourish. "I hope you will take these in good faith and wear them many times."

"Oh, Thomas." Awe wove through her voice as she opened the box. The parure—a necklace, tiara, earbobs, and a bracelet—matched the ring he'd given to her upon their wedding.

"I know my mother would have encouraged you to wear them." The oval-shaped emeralds of varying sizes in each piece winked in the sunlight along with the tiny diamonds that surrounded each. "There are many times I can remember her wearing the set, and my father always gave her a certain secret look those evenings. I didn't understand why at the time, but now I do." Daring much, he cupped the side of her face, tilted her head up so that their gazes met. "There is something about seeing a woman dripping with jewels you've given her."

"To show ownership?" she quipped with a trace of sarcasm in her tones.

"No." He couldn't help his grin, for if she was able to joke, she was feeling better. "To enhance a woman's beauty, so that she can go into society and show everyone she is valued, that she possesses looks enough to wear a king's ransom in jewels because the man in her life trusts her and wishes to show his adoration." It was a nodcock thing to say and didn't explain how he was beginning to feel at all, but he hoped she knew what he didn't say.

"They are gorgeous." She traced a few of the stones with a gloved fingertip. When Kip darted his head out from Thomas' greatcoat and licked the largest stone of the tiara, they both laughed. "And this jewelry will be perfect with the new gowns." Her chin trembled as she glanced up at him. "I have never owned anything nearly as valuable. Thank you."

He nodded. "You are quite welcome." The longer he looked at her, the more he feared he was rapidly changing without giving himself permission to do so. His world continued to shift about him while he stood there in shock and perhaps a bit of awe as the possibilities reordered before him. Where he never thought he had a future due to hiding in his past, Olivia had come along and ripped the blinders from his eyes. She'd yanked him from his comfortable cave and made him realize there was still life to live, and if he didn't, he was naught but a nodcock.

With another brush of her fingertips over the parure, she closed the box and uttered another sigh. "Did you wish to remain here or return home and have tea?"

"Warmth would be lovely." When he rose to his feet, he set Kip on the ground and took hold of the leather lead. "Our driver should have circled back through by now." When he glanced across the Serpentine, a stab of disappointment went through his chest, for Sally and her family had gone away while he'd been caught up in Olivia's story and heartbreak.

If that wasn't a metaphor for his life, he didn't know what was.

In no time at all, he saw her settled into the carriage and asked the driver to return them home. As soon as he sat on his bench, his wife joined him and sat beside him, leaving the dog on the opposite bench with the box of jewels. Before he could question her, she scooted close, slipped a hand to his nape, urged his head down, and then she pressed her lips to his in a gentle kiss. It was the first one she'd initiated, and the unexpected intimacy had need lancing down his spine to lodge in his stones. When she pulled back, she continued to hold his gaze with her lips slightly parted as if waiting for his reaction.

With a sigh of acceptance mixed with a soft groan, he slipped his arms about her and claimed her lips in a kiss designed to thank her, to show her that he wanted to see where their future would lead, to tell her he was willing to do whatever it took to make their union something she would be proud to enjoy.

There was nothing overtly erotic about the embrace. It was merely a comfortable exchange of respect and a way to bond with each other, and perhaps it was the first time since Cynthia that he'd kissed a woman without the overture heading into something sexual. When he pulled away, Olivia settled close to his side, and they passed the remainder of the ride in companionable silence.

Damn, but he could grow far too used to this. *What the devil do I do now?* For if it was true and he was falling for his wife, he didn't want to cock it up, but also knowing himself, he suspected that he would. It was merely a matter of time.

Chapter Twelve

December 22, 1817

Olivia shivered. She set down her knitting to pull the shawl more tightly about her shoulders. Wind gusts blew against the windows, and the veriest hint of snowflakes pinged at the glass. It wasn't enough precipitation to cover the ground by any stretch and would no doubt turn back into rain at some point during the night, but it was lovely to think about.

"Shall I ring for a footman to build up the fire?"

The sound of Thomas' baritone sent a host of flutters through her lower belly. She glanced across the low table at him where he lounged with his legs crossed at the knee on a sofa that matched in the private parlor on the second floor. "There is no need. Something about the wind makes it both cozy and concerning at the same time." The evergreen boughs that had been brought in to decorate the room filled the space with the fresh, pungent scent of pine, while clove-speckled oranges accentuated it with spice.

Kip, the traitorous dog, decided the viscount was a much more snuggly partner than she at the moment, for he lay curled up on the cushion beside him.

They'd had dinner a few hours ago and instead of retiring or moving into the drawing room, they'd decided mutually to make use of the smaller parlor. Candles about the room guttered in their holders and reflected off the scattering of tin bells nestled within the greenery. One of the servants had even seen fit to hang a bouquet of mistletoe in front of the window, tied off with a cheerful red ribbon. The fire danced merrily behind a decorative iron grate. Every so often, the coals would shift, releasing a spray of sparks that brought another layer of hominess to the scene. In her lap rested a pile of knitting, for she'd selected a jaunty, red-colored wool and was crafting a muffler for Thomas. She would give it to him on Christmas, probably at breakfast, for everyone needed help keeping warm during the season.

"I quite agree." He methodically folded his copy of *The Times* then laid the paper on a small table at his elbow. "Do you want tea or perhaps a glass of wine?"

The poor man was all too solicitous, but she secretly reveled in it. "Not at the moment." She started on the next row with her knitting. "Do we have plans for Christmas evening? If not, my brother would like to see me at dinner, and I would like for you to come as well."

After they'd returned home yesterday from the outing to Hyde Park, she'd been emotionally drained but somehow, she felt lighter for the telling of the remainder of her tale. And he had trusted her with the secret he'd been keeping as well. That alone had nearly laid her low, but bonding in shared grief had changed something between them. Their relationship had shifted, in a myriad of tiny ways, and now suddenly a future glimmered where there was once a wall.

They'd enjoyed tea together where Thomas had kept her entertained with stories from his salad days and all the trouble he and Pennington had fallen into. She had added stories of her own, that her father had told her of his time in Ireland. The discussion had moved to the land of her father's birth and whether she would ever go there for a visit, to pay homage to him. Truthfully, she didn't know if she ever wished to step foot in Ireland for all the trouble and angst it had brought to her family, but there was a tiny yearning deep in her soul to see that beautiful land.

Though they had ended the evening with another bout of kissing, she hadn't invited him into her bed, and he hadn't pushed for the same. Intercourse for the sake of a physical release didn't hold the same appeal it once had, and despite her seeing him in a different light and losing pieces of her heart to her husband, she couldn't quite let herself complete the fall.

Yet what did she wait for? Hadn't he already proved he was a kind and decent man? Hadn't he shown her that he would always take care of her, provide for her, give her the life and the dreams she'd always wanted?

Not knowing, she glanced at him only to find him watching her with a faint smile curving his lips. "What?"

"I answered your question, but you were so lost in thought you never responded."

"Oh." Warmth flooded her cheeks. "Tell me again."

"Pennington and his wife have invited us to dinner on Christmas Eve. I would like to attend, if only for the honor of having you on my arm."

That dratted charm of his! A butterfly ballet erupted in her belly. Was he only doing that to keep the peace, or did he truly wish to make inroads into beginning a life with her? Pretty words and his gift from yesterday were all too easy to falsify, and men lied without provocation. Still, she was flattered and did nothing to stop the freefall happening. "It will be lovely to see them again. Lady Pennington is an interesting person."

"Their romance is quite a story. Perhaps she will tell it to you."

"Were they matched because of the Lyon's Den?"

"Indeed, and Pennington fought tooth and nail against it, but eventually, Adriana tamed him, turned him from the beast that he was into a man more vastly approachable. He nearly lost her to the owner—Mrs. Dove-Lyon's—machinations, though."

"I never knew that." Truthfully, she had never heard of the Lyon's Den gaming hell until Conor had wagered and lost her hand at one of its tables. "I wonder if the woman thinks our union will ultimately fail." In a remote part of her mind, Olivia refused to give Mrs. Dove-Lyon the satisfaction of winning.

"Who can say? She has always remained mysterious and never shares her thoughts with anyone outside of her close circle." Thomas shrugged. "However, it is fascinating what the love of a good woman can do. If Mrs. Dove-Lyon is truly a matchmaker, she certainly must possess some sort of sorcery to have so many successful couples to her credit."

Her eyebrows rose in surprise. "She has matched more people than your friend and us?"

"Oh, yes. It is something of a tongue-in-cheek joke throughout the *ton*. And she usually uses trickery to make said matches come about." When he chuckled, the sound tickled through her insides. "The men are made to pay out the nose for the 'privilege' of being immediately matched and wed, and the women are almost always steeped in scandal of some sort."

"I suppose people with sterling reputations wouldn't step foot inside a gaming hell to begin with." Though knowing all of that lessened the sting of being forced to wed. "That doesn't reflect well on the women. It sounds as if the Lyon's Den is their last hope for securing a match of any kind." Is that how he looked at her, then? Even if Conor had lost her hand at a gaming table?

"That largely depends on the woman, wouldn't you say?" There was an intensity about him she didn't quite understand. "Scandalous women, in my opinion, are hardly that. It is merely a catch-all term society brands them with to explain the unexplainable. In fact, they are more likely opinionated, strong-willed, know their own mind, will fight for what they want, and are courageous as hell. How does any of that equate to being scandalous?"

Was he trying to appear adorable, or was she beginning to see him in such a light because she genuinely enjoyed being with him as time went on? Truly, they had both been misunderstood and had spent too long hiding from their grief.

"I rather like your explanation." If the owner of the gaming hell was gifted with a sort of second sight regarding matching couples, perhaps she'd seen something in Olivia's own union that had warranted the forced engagement. "In the end, it doesn't matter. You and I are wed, but I will tell you this." She met his gaze. "I will not give her a reason to doubt us. If she is, indeed, taking wagers against our union, she will lose. I don't suffer fools gladly, and if this woman thinks to antagonize me, she is foolish indeed." She didn't care how well-received or powerful this Mrs. Dove-Lyon was within society. Her roots ran deep, and she could prove a force to reckon with if provoked.

Surprise jumped into his eyes, but that slow, almost wicked grin caused her heart to flutter. "It is good to have your ire focused on someone other than me, but yes, I wholeheartedly agree with you."

For a bit, she continued knitting in silence while Kip's occasional snoring punctuated the quiet. Every so often, she would catch Thomas staring at her, and when she couldn't stand the attention any longer, she once more laid her project in her lap. "Why do you continue watching me? Surely, I cannot be that interesting."

"You would be surprised, and I find the act of knitting—or observing it—soothing. Something about the pull of the yarn and the gentle clack of the needles." He shrugged, but nothing about his body language suggested he was repentant. "I'm sorry I don't have a ball or rout planned for the holiday season. I hadn't expected to find myself married during this time, and even if I hadn't—"

"You would have hidden yourself away, drinking yourself into oblivion so you wouldn't remember all that you'd left behind," she interrupted in a soft voice. The fact he hadn't been as inebriated as he had been on their wedding night showed promise. She didn't begrudge a man his vices as long as it didn't endanger his life, ruin hers, or empty his coffers.

"Perhaps." His lips twitched with the beginnings of a grin. "In any event, I'm sure there are a few invitations on my desk in the study if you would like to go out into society for the first time as my viscountess."

Mmm, to tempt him downstairs and into the study. Would he make use of the desk like he had before? The thought almost carried her away and put another round of heat into her cheeks. "I would rather pass the holiday season quietly. Going to dinner with your friends and my brother is enough at the moment. Though…"

"Yes?" One of his blond eyebrows rose in challenge.

"I will miss having the opportunity to dance. It is one of the only things I enjoy about being in society." Where had that admission come from? She didn't like society at all, but in this case, she would have adored being partnered with *him*.

"Ah. I think I can be of assistance then." He clambered to his feet, edged around the table, and then offered her his hand with a theatrical flourish. "Lady Ashbury, will you do me the honor of sharing a waltz with me?"

The unexpected gallantry and romance of his question got the better of her and a giggle escaped. Olivia set aside her knitting. "We don't have music for accompaniment."

"Do we truly need it?" The wicked twinkle was back in his eyes. A tiny thrill buzzed at the base of her spine.

"No, I don't suppose we do." As soon as she slipped her fingers into his palm, he closed his around hers, and brought her swiftly to her feet. "What prompted this? I never would have thought you were a man who enjoyed such exercise." Especially since he'd been so maudlin of late.

"I do with the right partner." Then he led her away from the furniture, and while Kip watched with sleepy interest, he tugged her into his arms, the position much more scandalous than they could have achieved on a ballroom floor. "In an effort to not crash into the furniture, I'm forced to hold you close."

How could she not grin? Her heart squeezed. "Why, Ashbury, never say you're flirting with me." Olivia looked at Kip, who stared back as if he couldn't understand the human rituals that might lead to romance.

"I thought to try something different." For the space of a few heartbeats, his expression turned all too sober. "Perhaps it's time to discover if I can court happiness again."

As she stared at him with a bit of shock, he set them into motion, and what was more, he softly hummed the melody of a popular waltz against the shell of her ear. With every turn of the parlor, she tumbled faster down the slope, and if she didn't stop the fall, she would end up going tip over tail for her husband.

There were certainly worse things than being in love, but was he what she wanted? Could she see herself by his side for the remainder of her life? As she peered up into his face, met his gaze, trembled on the edge of those brandy-hued pools, she suddenly had the feeling that this was exactly where she'd always been meant to be.

With a tiny sigh, Olivia slipped a hand along his shoulders to his nape and let the other one rest upon his chest as he twirled her about the room. Not since she was a child when she'd pretended she was a fairy princess and that her prince would come swooping out of the woods to rescue her had she felt like she did now. There was something all too magical about being safe in Thomas' arms as the soothing timbre of his voice echoed in her ears. He might not be a prince and he might still be haunted by his past, but he was all too lovely, and if she closed her eyes, so easily could let herself be carried away with his charm and the way he was trying to be the man she wanted.

For that, she loved him.

With a tiny gasp, her eyes flew open, and she met his gaze. Was that true? Surely, she couldn't have fallen so quickly for a man she barely knew and had hated upon first sight. Then he smiled at her for no other reason than he was enjoying himself, and her heart fluttered again.

Oh dear. It would seem I'm in a bit of trouble.

Without a word, he led her over the floor to the window and maneuvered her beneath the sprigs of mistletoe. "Here's to seeing Christmastide in a whole different light," he whispered as he cupped her cheek and then kissed her lips with a tenderness that brought tears to her eyes.

How much did she want this man? Lifting onto her toes, she looped her arms about his shoulders and kissed him back, taking little nips and nibbles from his lips until he caught her up into his embrace, held her impossibly close, and then took full advantage of deepening the embrace. A rush of desire surged through her, and though she wanted nothing more than to take him to bed, she needed to be all too sure their union would last.

After a few heated moments and far too many delicious kisses that left them both breathless, Thomas pulled away. "Should we adjourn upstairs?"

A shaky laugh escaped her. "I am not ready." Would he think her playing coy since they had already come together intimately? "After so much has happened…"

"Shh." He scooped up one of her hands and brought it to her lips. "Out of everyone in London, I understand all too well." A trace of sadness went through his expression, and her heart trembled. Did he feel as she did? If so, why hadn't he admitted to it? For that matter, why wouldn't she? "Perhaps I should read to you from some of my favorite poets—Keats, Byron, or even Cowper."

She swallowed around the wad of emotion stuck in her throat. "I would enjoy that very much." The words came out in a whisper, and she hated herself for the lack of courage to confess to her emotions first. Once more she was hiding, not behind grief or anger this time, but of fear. What if she told him what was in her heart, and he rejected her outright? What if he told her that he could never love another woman, just as he'd maintained at their nuptial ceremony? After all, they hadn't been wed long. Love took time, didn't it?

"Good." He was everything courtly and charming as he led her back to the grouping of furniture, but instead of sitting on the sofa from before, he pulled her down on one closer to the fire, encouraged her to lay upon the length with her head resting in his lap. "I think we shall begin with Lord Byron. Nice chap, so I've been told."

Then she was lost to the rumble of his voice and the comfortable solidness of him beneath her head.

What am I to do now after I have spent so many years hating him and wanting revenge? Was it acceptable to change her mind or to even admit she had been wrong?

There was much to think about.

Chapter Thirteen

December 23, 1817

An hour after teatime found Thomas at his club searching out Simon. His mind was conflicted, so much so that talking to the captain might give him comfort or insight. He would have called on Pennington, but since he was to see the earl on the morrow, he sought out the counsel of his other best friend instead.

As always, Simon sat negligently in a chair with a glass of brandy in hand and a copy of one of London's many newspapers in the other. He was certainly dashing and enigmatic in the candlelight, since it was a gray and cold afternoon with fat gray clouds that might portend snow. When he glanced up and caught sight of Thomas, his eye widened.

"I am surprised to see you here, Ashbury. Now that you're married, I thought your time was well and truly spoken for, or you turned tail and retreated back to your country estate." He chuckled at his own joke. "Rumor holds that your new wife is quite the handful."

"That, my friend, is an understatement," he mumbled as he more or less collapsed into the chair beside Simon's. With a sigh, he rubbed a hand along the side of his face. "However, after a rather interesting and frightening start to our union, things have leveled off." The impromptu dance from yesterday that had led to kissing then poetry reading still left him stunned. It had been far too domestic and all too easy to want to usher in more of the same into his life. "Which is why I'm left at sixes and sevens."

"Regarding what?" The captain took a sip of his brandy. "You either rub along well with the woman or you don't."

Truly, the man wasn't helpful. Thomas rolled his gaze heavenward for a second. "After everything, I think I might be falling in love with my wife." He lowered his voice as Simon stared in shock. "However, doing so terrifies me."

"Why?"

"For one, I don't know if I wish to put myself through all of that again in the event something dire happens."

"That is understandable after the last time you gave out your heart." Simon's eyebrow rose in challenge. "But is what you feel for your wife truly love, or is it merely infatuation like before, when I suspect you were in love with the idea of being in love and having a romance? Especially since that relationship infuriated your father."

Never would he live that down. A sigh escaped him. "If I'm being honest with myself, this time feels... different." There was no other way to explain it. "Since I married Olivia, I have had cause to think."

"I have already cautioned you against such folly," the captain said with a sardonic grin.

"Oh, indeed, but think I did. Ennui and being lost to the past are no way to live. By hook or by crook, the woman has yanked me out of the muck and demanded that I face my demons."

"And?"

He huffed. "And she is different from Cynthia in every way. She's brash and outspoken and despite her wishing to kill me on sight, we have shared confidences, have been able to talk through the things that have tried to break us, and I've shared my fears as well as shortcomings."

Simon tapped a forefinger against the side of his glass. "Which still doesn't explain anything of consequence to me."

"No, I suppose it doesn't, but instead of the idealistic future I assumed I would have with Cynthia, what I can have instead with Olivia is... awe-inspiring. It's real." He glanced at his friend, held his gaze, willed him to understand. "What I feel goes deeper than anything ever has before. I want everything that life with a wife entails, even a family and perhaps an heir, regardless of whether those children will be as my first."

"I beg your pardon, but your first? You have a child?" The captain's lower jaw dropped open after incredulity rang in his whispered inquiry.

Quickly, Thomas gave him an overview of his life to this point, and why it concerned the hell out of him. Then he sat back and waited for usable advice.

"You have managed to render me speechless. However, your willingness to move forward despite the obstacles in quite inspiring."

"Thank you." Some of the pressure in his chest lessened from those words. "I still feel as if I'll cock everything up."

The captain snorted. "No doubt you will."

"What?"

"Just this." Simon sat up straighter in his chair. "Any man in your position would do the same, for the stakes in the relationship will raise. You will have to decide between the past and her. There is no more room for waffling, for hiding."

Though he'd known this day was coming, Thomas hadn't been prepared to meet it so soon. "We have only been married for six days, and the first two I was trying to avoid being murdered." He shook his head. "How is love even possible in such a short span?"

"Perhaps it is not. Perhaps it is. Love is both fickle and wonderous. I rather doubt any of us understand it fully."

That wasn't helpful, and when did the captain become a philosopher of riddles? "What if I am not good at being a husband?"

"It is a skill you will learn, just as countless other men before you have."

He blew out a breath. "And if I fail?" he asked in a small voice as knots of worry pulled in his gut.

"Then you continue to ask for forgiveness, or you can send her to the country where you can resume your former life." The captain shrugged. "To my way of thinking, it is not a question for the ages."

"That is because you have never grappled with the problem of loving someone to distraction and knowing your own history of failure." Thomas frowned as Simon folded his newspaper and set it aside. "After talking over my history with Olivia, I don't believe I wish to return to that misery, to being the bitter and angry man of before."

The captain's eyebrow rose again, this time in surprise. The emotion reflected in his expression. "Are you better with her?"

Was he? She certainly made him think, and she challenged him at every turn. Olivia made him look at the world differently. There was nothing complicated about her, nothing that he had to work overly hard at to discover. Though he didn't know all of what she dreamed about or knew of her goals in life, he wanted to take a slow lifetime to discover everything.

Suddenly, he grinned, felt almost giddy if that were possible. "Yes, and that frightens me as well."

Simon chuckled. "Then, my friend, you are truly in love, and there is no hope for your rehabilitation."

"I suppose you are quite correct." But it didn't sound like the prison sentence that he'd originally thought. He snickered. "Damn."

"Indeed." The captain drained the brandy left in his glass. "Have you told her of your feelings?"

"Not yet. I only came to the realization recently."

"Then why are you here with me?" Simon shook his head with a grin. "Go home and tell her. Claim her body as many times as she will let you and stay in bed until Pennington's dinner tomorrow. Then you can regale us both with your erotic tales."

Heat crept up the back of Thomas' neck. "I thought you were against marriage."

"I am—for me—but the holiday makes me maudlin, and I think I might like to have that someday." He shrugged and a wicked light twinkled in his eye. "And then, I tell myself I'm thinking too much and call for another brandy."

Weren't they all just searching for that, to be themselves, to stave off loneliness, to be understood and loved unconditionally and not be alone?

"Truthfully, though, I wish you good fortune." The captain's expression sobered. "You are the best of us, and no one deserves to live that dream more than you."

"Thank you." God, that humbled the hell out of him. A ball of emotion rose into his throat, so he stood in an effort to hide that reaction. "I hope you soon find what it is you are looking for in this life as well."

And would that his friend didn't learn until it was too late as he had.

WHEN THOMAS ARRIVED home, the wind had kicked up and thrown a few snow flurries through the rapidly darkening air. Truly, it was a foul night, and he was all too grateful he'd planned to spend it inside, hopefully with his wife.

Eventually, he'd found her in the library. Kip lay curled on the floor before the fireplace. The golden glow of candles throughout the room gave the space a homy feeling that he hadn't known since before his mother had died. But it was Olivia herself that made his breath catch.

"Why are you dressed so finely? Are we going out?"

Clad in a silver satin gown with some sort of mesh overskirt that twinkled with silver thread and clear glass beads, she was a vision, but her glorious, fiery hair had been left unbound. It rippled down her back in gentle waves, and was like burnished copper where the firelight touched it. Instead of expensive gems about her neck, she only wore a pink enamel rose on a silver chain. The very simplicity of the bauble was fitting and encouraged his gaze to linger at her décolletage, for the wash of golden freckles only enhanced the swell of her breasts over the low bodice.

She rose slowly to her feet, dropping the book that had been open on her lap. It fell to the Aubusson carpeting with a dull thud. "We are not. I thought dinner tonight should be festive but between the two of us since we have plans to go out for the next two evenings." Uncertainty clouded her gray eyes. "Dinner will be served in a couple of hours, or so Wallace says. Do you, uh, like the gown? It's one of the new ones."

Finally, he remembered how to breathe, and like the nodcock that he was, Thomas nodded. "It is amazing, as if you fell from the heavens." His feet felt rooted to the floor. Why couldn't he move?

"I adore that kind of compliment." Olivia closed the distance between them, but then she went past him a few steps and softly closed the door behind them before turning to regard him again. "You look as if you have had a revelation and it's shaken you."

"Perhaps I have, so it is fortuitous I've found you here, for I wanted to talk with you privately." Dear God, why wouldn't the words come? They sat at the tip of his tongue but went nowhere.

"Oh?" Concern immediately clouded her eyes. "Is all well?"

"I believe so." He maneuvered his body so that he fully faced her.

"You see, I think..." Why the devil couldn't he force out the words? What an idiot. His beautiful wife stood before him in a fantastic gown looking like twelve kinds of sin, yet he couldn't tell her what was in his heart? Cold fear twisted down his spine. The last time he'd told a woman he'd loved her, it had ended horribly. "I... I was never good with words," he finally said, and took refuge in cowardice.

For the space of a few heartbeats, she held his gaze while he struggled, wished the floor would swallow him whole. Finally, she nodded, took his hand, and led him away from the door. "I understand."

"You do?"

"Yes." Olivia laid a hand on his chest. "Sometimes, Ashbury, there is no need for words." Then she stood on her toes and pressed her petal-soft lips to his.

That tiny overture set fire to his blood and sent every thought from his head except the need to claim her, show her with his body how much he was coming to adore her.

As she drank from him as if he held the last drop of water on Earth, he followed her lead. Dear God, but she was both heaven and hell in his arms, and with some awe, he let her command the embrace, for she devoured him as if she had no decorum at all. When she dragged her lips down the column of his throat, a shuddering sigh issued from him.

"I want you, Olivia."

"Then perhaps we should shed some clothing and go from there, hmm?" Her smile could tempt even the most devout religious man into sin.

Never had he relieved himself of his clothes so quickly. Each piece landed indiscriminately on the floor, and the second he tossed his breeches away, he gladly played maid to her. The laces at the back of her sparkling gown fell away to his questing fingers. It took less time than a sigh for the gown to puddle on the floor at her feet while Kip lazily watched their antics before returning to slumber. Her stays only slowed him slightly; her petticoat and shift yielded far too easily to his enthusiasm.

Then she was as naked as he, but her alabaster skin was the stuff of dreams, and the freckles were flecks of gold in the candlelight. Damn, how long would it take to count every single one? And more to the point, did she have them everywhere? He didn't know but he would discover that and soon.

"No dagger tonight?" There was nothing strapped to her thigh, and all he could think about was pressing kisses to that silky skin.

"Haven't you learned by now that I no longer wish to carve out your heart?" she asked in a soft voice with a wicked grin indeed.

Then she was back in his arms, and their kisses grew wilder and more passionate as time went on. Would she truly understand what he didn't say?

It didn't matter. In this moment, she would truly be his wife, for he wanted her in all the ways a man could, and if showing her such took all night, so be it. His appetite had fled regardless. When he tried to catch her into his arms to move them to a sofa, she shook her head and winked.

"Not yet, Ashbury." Olivia slid down his body, touching and caressing his skin as she went until she kneeled before him, so perilously close to his throbbing member he held his breath. "I wish to give you pleasure before you command this embrace."

Hellfire and damnation. The woman means to kill me after all.

"I don't suppose I'll bid you nay, for you are far too fascinating that I cannot wait to see what you'll do next." It was true. She had well and truly caught him in her spell.

"How strong is your stamina before you will break?" Up and down, she drew her hand along his shaft with her curled fingers about the thick girth.

With every stroke, his grip on reality threatened to separate. Awareness shivered over him, and he stood captive, powerless to her intent. Each brush of her fingers on his aching rod quickened his pulse and his breathing, for she was like magic. Yet he widened his stance, as much to give her more room to work with as to keep himself upright. "Perhaps you should leave off." Strain graveled his voice.

"Where is the fun in that? I want you hovering desperately on the edge for me, as payback for the times you did the same to me." With a slow grin, Olivia came forward, and as if she had all the time in the world, she licked the wide head of his shaft.

"Olivia!" His hiss of warning echoed in the silence of the room.

Her only response was a giggle. She continued to work him over with her hand while taking his length into her mouth, and that warmth around his shaft nearly became his undoing.

"Damn it all." Not knowing what else to do, he buried one of his hands in the heavy mass of her hair, encouraged her as close as he dared.

She hummed around him, apparently enjoying every second of torturing him, and when she moved her hand down to cup his stones, his body twitched. His breathing became ragged while she applied various degrees of depth and suction to his erect member, alternately squeezing his stones and returning to twist her fingers around his shaft.

"Please, leave off." The whisper was lost to a moan, and of course the woman didn't follow his command, for she licked the underside of his appendage, slipped a hand behind him to squeeze a buttock. "Argh!" His wife ignored his outcry. She took him once more into her mouth, bobbing up and down on him, faster and faster. As she did, she held him steady with a hand at his thigh. He was nearly out of his mind as he fisted both hands into her hair, thrust into her mouth in time to the rhythm she'd set, and when she trailed her other hand to that stretch of skin between his stones and anus, everything went into sharp relief. Need shot down his length and made his stones tingle.

"Olivia, enough!" Desperation propelled the soft cry. He pulled out of her mouth before things ended far too soon. He grabbed hold of her upper arms and yanked her unceremoniously to her feet. "I'm going to explode."

Her mussed hair, her swollen lips, the faint splotches of red on her face and chest that spoke to her own arousal stole his ability to think. "That is quite the point of this exercise."

"Agreed, but I'll be damned if I do it down your throat."

"You are quite the romantic. Must be all the poetry you read." With a smile, she lifted onto her toes and brushed her lips over his. "I rather think it's adorable." Olivia kissed him again with more pressure and held his gaze the whole time, waiting, watching, daring him to make the next move.

How damned lucky was he to have married her?

"Vixen." Thomas wrapped his arms around her and returned her kiss with more passion than finesse. She'd already teased him to the point of losing control, and as his aching, hard length pressed against her belly, he couldn't postpone the inevitable.

Not that he wanted to. Tonight, he would tell her with his body how much he was coming to adore her, to love her, that he was thankful she'd come into his life.

With a shuddering sigh as she looped her arms about his shoulders, he settled her more comfortably in his arms and applied himself to the task of making her forget her own name. He nibbled her bottom lip, licked the plump flesh, nipped at the corner of her mouth. When her hands twined behind his nape, the movement pressed her breasts into his chest, and they both moaned. Needing much more from her, he took full advantage and pushed his tongue inside her mouth to fence with hers.

His pulse pounded in his ears. Heat rolled over him. Desire lanced through him. He slid a hand down her back to her arse and walked her backward until one of the shelves prevented further movement. As his length throbbed, he ground his hips into hers, but the additional friction didn't alleviate the need. "You feel so damned good." Thomas gripped her waist and lifted her, never breaking contact with her mouth, and pressed her against the wall to keep her upright. A few books fell to the floor at his feet with dull thuds.

"You feel even better. So strong and hard in all the right places." The maddening woman nipped a line of kisses beneath his jaw. "Plus, you are intelligent and caring. A heady mixture, and one not readily found in a man of the *ton*." Her gaze fell to the plain, thin, silver ring he wore on a thin cord about his neck, but she didn't question him.

Reminding himself to explain all, he pinched her arse cheek. "Perhaps you haven't been looking in the right places. Men like me exist."

"But are hiding?" Arching an eyebrow, she grinned. "Take me, Ashbury. Let there be no more uncertainty between us."

Did that mean she felt the same as he? He didn't know, but her pink nipples stood erect and called out to him. He took one of those tips into his mouth while she wrapped a hand about his nape and guided him closer. One swipe of his tongue along the pebbled bud had her squirming. A second one made her back arch and gave him greater access. As her fingers went into his hair, he was lost.

He explored her satiny skin with his tongue, licking all around the puckered flesh before sucking the point back into his mouth. When she vibrated with need, he switched his attention to the other bud. With the books at her back, the flush of desire over her face, and her fingers at her own nipple, squeezing, twisting it to further enhance his ministrations, he nearly came right there. Then he redoubled his efforts to bring her to the edge she'd just had him on.

"Give me more."

Oh, but they would have such fun together. Desire flooded his senses and guided his instincts. He cupped her lush breasts. The mounds filled his hands, and he pushed the pillowy masses together, pressed his face into them, rubbed his cheeks and chin against them so his stubble would scrape and tease—mark her. When she gasped, he tweaked the swollen nipples and rolled them before once more torturing them with his mouth, teeth, and tongue.

"Mmm, yes."

Lost and never wanting to find his way back, Thomas kissed her with a savagery that surprised them both, but his wife gave as good as she got, and that further worked to separate him from his thoughts. When he couldn't maintain the contact he wanted, he slid his hands beneath her buttocks and lifted her, and she locked her ankles at the small of his back. A few more books tumbled from the shelves, but he didn't care. Never had those volumes looked as good as they did on the floor and providing a backdrop from the naked, redhaired woman in his arms.

"Send me flying, Thomas." The breathy way she said it preceded him slipping a hand between them by mere seconds. He slid his fingers past her mons and then into the curls at the apex of her thighs. Finally, when he explored her flesh slick with arousal, encouraged the swollen button at her center out of hiding, they both sighed. "This is madness. You have bewitched me." And he kissed her while working to send her over the edge into bliss.

Her breathing shallowed, and her fingers dug into his shoulders, the nails bringing pinpricks of pain that only enhanced the pleasure swirling through him. "More. I want to feel it, feel you inside me."

"So damned needy." He transferred his grip to her thighs, pressed her harder against the shelf of books, hefting her up, her weight slight in his hold, but he fit the tip of his member to her opening. "I rather like you desperate for me." With tiny teasing movements, he stroked into her passage but didn't quite penetrate her, for he wished to taunt and torment first.

"Bastard." She wriggled and then moaned as she gripped his shoulders to stay upright. "Don't make me fetch my dagger."

"Ah, coitus by knifepoint. That does have a certain intrigue about it." The woman would drive him into madness, but at least he would enjoy the trip. When she feathered light kisses to the underside of his jaw, his ability to think completely left him.

He claimed her lips again, drank from her, shared long drugging kisses with her, and when he speared his tongue into her mouth, he thrust into her lush, hot body, and didn't stop until he was fully seated, and she was trapped between him and the shelf of books behind her.

Their moans blended together.

Heady sensations raced up his length to tingle in his stones. "I adore this moment."

"As do I." She cupped his cheek with one hand while the other curled about his nape. In his ear, she whispered, "Send me flying…" Her words drifted off as he moved within her, and every damned stroke drove him closer to the point of no return.

But he didn't care, for she was his wife, now and forever, and they had a whole lifetime to explore each other in this way. A purely primal grin curved his mouth, yet he still had no words, so he merely kissed her, told her with his actions how he felt. Primed to the point of explosion, he stroked in and out at a fast pace and each time, her body gripped him, welcomed him in with heat and wonder… welcomed him home.

Oh, God.

To prevent himself from fumbling, from letting emotions distract his purpose, he claimed her body, penetrated her as if this would be the last time. Deeper. Faster. Harder. Every thrust sucked him under waves of building need. Each push hurtled him closer to the edge of oblivion.

"Oh, yes!" Olivia tightened her ankles about his waist, which encouraged him inside her so much that he feared he'd lose himself. Her fingernails would no doubt leave crescents on his skin and the soft sounds she made at the back of her throat in encouragement and enthusiasm left him shuddering with the need to give in to bliss.

"I won't last. Can't…" Already, the need to spend tingled through his stones and rushed through his shaft. He was done for. With nothing else to do, he shoved his hand between their bodies to play at her swollen pearl, teasing it with varying degrees of desperate friction while continuing to thrust as books left the shelf to hit the floor.

Olivia gasped. She met his gaze, held it, and he swore a piece of his soul went into her keeping while she gave him the same in that shared moment. Her hips bucked as she tried to follow his rhythm, but in the end, she merely bit the crook of his shoulder as her whole body stiffened. "Oh!" A cry left her throat. She dug her fingers into his skin, and while he stroked another few times as her body spasmed around his shaft, she shattered in his arms. A few more books fell to the floor.

Seconds later, with a shout, Thomas followed. The release collected him into its vortex, and he came so damned hard he gasped from his own reaction to the coupling. Stars burst behind his closed eyelids, and this time he didn't pull out of her body before his seed emptied. For better or for worse, they were now joined for life.

With a groan, he collapsed into her, held her steady between his chest and the bookshelf while his breathing and hers rasped into the quiet of the room, punctuated with the crackle and pop of the fire. It was his responsibility to keep her content and happy, to continue to share his life with her, and perhaps something wonderful would come from this second chance.

Suddenly, he wanted to marry her again, write supplemental vows, say them to her from his heart this time instead of repeating dusty old words that had been said with vitriol and hatred at their first nuptial ceremony.

For a true new beginning. Resolute, he claimed her lips in a gentle kiss then pressed his lips to her sweat-damp forehead. He would ask Pennington's advice regarding his plan tomorrow at dinner.

Olivia held his face between her palms and met his gaze. "I think I know what you wanted to say when you came in."

His heartbeat accelerated. "Do you want me to confirm it with words?" He would do that for her, but preferred making the grand gesture with the second ceremony.

"Not quite yet." Her smile was tired. Exhaustion reflected in her eyes. "Not until *I'm* sure."

"Very well." Thomas nodded. Perhaps she needed more time. He couldn't fault her for that. "Do you want me to go?" Slowly, gently, as if she were the most valuable thing, he released her, guided her feet to the floor.

"No. Stay here with me for tonight. Allow me a chance to rest, but I have so many other plans for you, now that we get on together." Wicked promise flashed in her eyes.

"Oh?" Well, damn.

"Very much so." She pressed her lips to the underside of his jaw, and renewed need shuddered through his shaft. Then she peered into his eyes. "Afraid?"

"God, yes." Was there too much truth in that admission?

"Good, then you won't be bored, and neither will your eyes wander." When Olivia wrapped her arms about him and kissed him, he was well and truly lost.

I am in love with my wife. It was quite surreal but exciting at the same time.

Chapter Fourteen

December 24, 1817
Christmas Eve

Olivia stretched with all the leisure and contentment of a cat. The pleasant ache in her muscles reminded her of the activity and exercise she and Thomas had indulged in last night. All night long and part of today, truth be told. In various positions and places throughout the library, until they'd fallen asleep out of necessity with breaks only for food, to take Kip out, or attend to other bodily needs that had nothing to do with coupling.

Now, as the longcase clock in the upstairs corridor chimed the six o'clock hour, she put the final stitches onto the muffler she'd made for Thomas and cast it off the needles. Oh, it would look so dapper and cheerful around his neck and peeking out from beneath his greatcoat. She only hoped he would wear it since it was made from a lower-class hobby.

An hour or so ago, he'd gone upstairs to bathe and dress for dinner at the Earl of Pennington's home. No doubt there would be parlor games and conversation along with fine wines and decadent sweets following dinner. It would be lovely spending time with people who knew her husband the best, and perhaps she could pick their brains and learn more about him.

At some point last night, he'd told her why he wore that silver band around his neck, for it had been the band he'd hoped to give Cynthia on the day they were to wed, but the baby coming early had rendered those dreams moot. He'd admitted that he'd worn it out of habit, for it was a means of never forgetting. Now that he was coming out of the need to hide within his past or use it as a crutch, he said he probably should put it away into a box and truly move forward.

She had listened with the proper sympathy and respect, for she still missed her friend terribly, but there was something to be said for ushering in a future that was beyond the grasping tendrils of the past. For the moment, she wouldn't push him to remove the ring, and she hoped he would do so by himself, but after the nearly twenty-four hours they'd spent together, she was nearly certain their marriage would flourish.

And that she was well and truly tip over tail for her husband. As a lifetime with him glimmered before her, Olivia couldn't wait to step onto that path beside him, learn everything there was to know about him, and forge new memories that would help heal both of their battered and bruised hearts.

"Olivia, are you still within?"

The sound of Thomas' voice stirred the butterflies in her belly, and she smiled as she tucked the finished muffler beneath a decorative pillow on the sofa along with a quick note she'd scribbled and then stood. "I am, but I should go upstairs and dress. We're due at Pennington's in an hour. I don't want to keep his wife waiting."

Then he came into the room. Immediately, the scents of sandalwood and citrus wafted to her nose and sent renewed awareness skittering over her skin. How could she want him—again—after they'd spent copious amounts of time together intimately already? Of course, they *were* in their honeymoon period…

"I wouldn't mind if you went like that." Dressed in evening clothes complete with tailcoat, he was so handsome she had to look twice at him. The waistcoat of crimson satin embroidered with tiny white snowflakes was an adorable nod to the holiday.

Heat seeped into her cheeks, for she'd donned an Oriental-style wrapper, procured during a midnight run through the house for provisions and supplies. "And have society brand me more scandalous than I already am?"

"As if I needed another reason to crow in front of my fellows about my wife?" The man advanced further into the room, caught her swiftly into his arms, and then proceeded to kiss her senseless, not letting her up for air until she'd been rendered well and truly breathless. When they parted, amusement and desire danced in his eyes. Oh, how she wanted to put her fingers through his blond hair and give it a good tousle, risking censure from his valet.

"Do hush, Ashbury." She gave his chest a playful swat, even if that kiss had ushered in a certain reaction to him. "I must run. Do me a favor and take Kip outside so he can do his business? And tell him what a good boy he's been, for we've rather neglected playing with him recently."

"Can I help it if I find you more fascinating to play with than your dog?" When she giggled, he winked. "Of course I'll take him out and let him walk in the garden. I have already asked Wallace to make certain the carriage is waiting at the curb in fifty minutes. Will that be enough time?"

"I shall do my best." Then she fled the room, because if she didn't, Olivia feared she might never leave the library or the addicting pull of her husband's kisses. Wholeheartedly, she trusted him, and the feelings tumbling through her heart made it seem her feet scarcely touched the floor as she made her way to the upper level and her suite. Being in love was rather exhilarating.

As expected, dinner with the Earl and Countess of Pennington was a lovely affair. Thomas' other friend Captain Huxley had also been in attendance, along with the countess' sister and their parents.

Conversation abounded, as did laughter, tricks, parlor games, and enough food and spirits to give heat to the cheeks and a fullness to the belly. By the time she and Thomas were bundled into their carriage for the ride home at half past eleven, and with light snow flurries drifting down and a brick to warm their feet beneath lap blankets, they were nearly asleep upon arrival.

Excitement buzzed through the air inside the house, for the staff was preparing to attend midnight services. Olivia had declined to go with them, for though she believed in God and was properly grateful for her life, she was of a mind that she didn't need to sit in a hard-backed pew or listen to a boring vicar drone on in order to talk to the Creator whenever she felt the urge. Besides, she'd rather usher in Christmas while wrapped in her husband's arms, snuggled in front of a fire where she could give him his gift in the privacy of their home.

"I'm going upstairs to check on Kip, perhaps take him out for one more walk before retiring," she said as she gave over her bonnet and cloak to Wallace, who waited in the entry hall.

"I need to fetch something from my study." He looked all too mysterious when he said that.

She nodded. "I'll look for you upstairs then, after I retrieve my knitting from the library." With a glance at Wallace, she smiled. "Have a lovely time at church tonight."

"I will. Thank you, my lady. Should I ring for tea before leaving?"

"No, thank you. If I'm in need, I shall go down to the kitchens myself." It was one skill she'd learned from an early age. "Be careful while you are out. It's snowing. Very lightly, but still, it could be slippery later."

"Thank you for the warning." He nodded at them both. "Enjoy your evening." Then, with a barely contained smirk, he went down the hall toward the servants' stairs.

Heat slapped at her cheeks, for there was no doubt in Olivia's mind that the servants were very much aware of what occurred last night between her and Thomas. "We are far too scandalous for our own good, I think," she whispered to him as she moved toward the main staircase.

"That doesn't bother me one whit." Then he made a playful swat at her bottom. "Don't be long. I haven't nearly had my fill of you yet, and I cannot wait to peel that gown from your body layer by layer."

"Oh!" The heat in her face intensified. It was the green gown with the glass beads she'd been wearing the first time they'd come together in the drawing room, only this time she'd paired a few pieces of the emerald parure with it. She glanced over her shoulder at him and couldn't help but quip, "Somehow, I rather doubt this will be a silent night."

"Ha!" An expression of joy crossed his face as he chuckled, and it was the most welcome sound. He hadn't had much cause to laugh over the course of their marriage, but she hoped he would do it more often. "There is so much unexpected... delight with you." Then he continued along the corridor while she made her way upstairs.

Not immediately locating the dog, she peered beneath pieces of furniture and called out his name, but he was definitely not in her suites. She waved goodbye to her maid and bid her a good night then continued on searching for Kip. When he didn't make an appearance in the viscount's suite, she moved downstairs and searched through the drawing room as well as the morning room. Each place was suspiciously silent and devoid of all life.

Thinking, perhaps, that he'd bedded down for the evening in the library where they had all spent copious amounts of time, Olivia popped in there next. Then she frowned. It was rather chilly in the room despite the heat from the fireplace. Her basket of knitting supplies reposed on the floor next to the sofa where she'd been working earlier. The pallet in front of the hearth was empty, and Kip was nowhere to be found in the room, but when she approached the French-paned doors that led out into the garden, she sucked in a breath. One of the doors stood open a handful of inches, just enough to admit a little dog into the outside world.

"Kip!" After dashing across the room, she threw open the door and stepped outside. The dog wasn't immediately seen in the walled off garden, but that meant nothing. He was a master of squirming through the smallest spaces to escape and explore. "Kip!" When an answering bark wasn't immediately heard, Olivia went back into the library. "Thomas!" The only heat in her voice this time was of anger. It jumped into her chest sure and swift as if it had never left. "Damn your eyes!"

Ashbury ran in with an expression of alarm. "What is it? What has happened?" He roved his gaze up and down her person. "Are you well?"

"No, I am not bloody well." As she passed her knitting basket, she yanked up her scissors, pulled them from their leather sheath, and then brandished the pair like the knife that it could be. "You dolt. You haven't the brains that God gave a goose. Look there." She pointed at the door with her blade. "You must not have secured the latch properly, for the door was open and Kip is gone!"

Immediately, shock sprang into his eyes. All joy faded from his face, only to be replaced by annoyance and fear. "How the hell do you know it was me who didn't secure the latch?"

"You were the last one in here, the person I'd tasked with taking Kip out for a walk before we left for dinner." She advanced upon him with the tip of her blade leading the way. How silly of her to think that every difference between them and the animosity could be forgotten by a few heady sessions between the sheets, satisfying though they'd been. "My dog is gone and there is no one to blame except you." Her hand shook, from anger or fear for Kip she couldn't say.

"If I didn't latch the door properly, I apologize, but instead of blaming me, why don't we look for Kip together?"

Of course what he said made sense, damn him. "You'd better hope we can find the dog. Otherwise, there will be hell to pay."

He snorted. Annoyance roiled off him in waves. "You'll go back to making my life miserable? Threatening me with your dagger? I'm sure the servants will have a *wonderful* time with that tittle-tattle!" Sarcasm lay heavy in his voice as he followed her across the room and then out into the garden.

The snow came down slightly harder than it had when they'd arrived home. "If that is what it takes to make you sorry."

A gasp left his throat. "For marrying you? Oh, we are already there."

Hurt stabbed through her heart. Had he meant those words or were they merely said in the heat of the moment? "Kip?" It was so dark in the garden. Not even the candlelight from within the library could illuminate much. "Where are you boy?"

Thomas, to his credit, walked the perimeter of the wall. "No good will come if we panic about this. I'm sure Kip didn't go far. He adores his warm, dry, well-fed life too much to strike out on his own in this weather."

"You'd better hope that's true." Her hand shook, for if she couldn't locate her dog, she would most certainly make a mark on her husband. As fear twisted up her spine, she darted hither and yon in the garden, regardless that her hem was getting wet, and her feet were growing colder by the second. "Kip, where are you?" She couldn't keep the alarm from her tone.

"I'm sorry, Olivia." Truly, that emotion sounded in his voice. It tugged at her heart. "Sorry for not checking the latch. Sorry for making it possible for Kip to escape, but anyone could have made that mistake." When she didn't answer, he huffed out his frustration. "Between you and I, we *will* find him."

Not wanting to be soothed in the moment while she was so worried, she shook her head. "There will be no you and I if we don't." She peered into a few bushes but the dog was clearly gone.

"What?" He stopped and stared at her in shock. "You would toss away all we have worked toward for the sake of a dog?"

Something inside her snapped. For the last week, she had been at the mercy of one emotion or the other, was told her brother was so careless that he'd gambled away her hand, had been forced to wed a man still in love with a ghost, and then had gone to battle against those same feelings for the man who'd she'd stupidly fallen in love with but hadn't the courage to say what was on her heart.

It was all too much.

"What do you not understand, Ashbury? That dog is like my baby," she said in a low tone that most in her circle would know meant trouble. When she was under heavy duress as she was in this moment, the Irish lilt became more prominent. "Kip was there for me when I lost Cynthia. He was there when I birthed a stillborn baby and was plunged into the most horrid grief I have ever known. He comforted me when I lost my parents, when my damned brother mucked about in my life and gave me over to you." She was shaking so badly from the cold and reaction that she dropped the scissors. "So yes, I am quite upset my dog is missing. Quite frankly, I don't know that I would shed a tear if you were gone in his stead. After all, you never wanted me anyway after Cynthia."

The words were said out of anger, out of fear, out of duress, and she immediately regretted them the second they'd been uttered. Even more so now that hurt lay stamped over his face. He staggered backward a few steps and clutched at his chest as if he sustained a mortal wound from a lance. His eyes, dear God, his eyes had darkened and were shadowed with so much hurt and betrayal, that it tore shreds from her own heart.

"Oh, Thomas, I didn't mean—"

He chopped at the air with a hand, interrupting her. All the color had faded from his face. "I rather don't wish to hear more," he said in a voice stilted and graveled with emotion. "How stupid of me to assume we had both laid our challenges—our fears—to rest but thank you for letting me know exactly where I stand with you." And still, he clutched his hand over his heart, for she had essentially ripped it out. "I shall make appropriate arrangements to ensure we need not see each other again."

It was on the tip of her tongue to spill out the contents of her heart, her soul, but the barking of a dog from somewhere in the square beyond the garden distracted her. "Kip!" Grabbing her skirting in her hands, she hiked it up and tore out of the garden by way of the wooden gate and ran into the square beyond. The snow chilled her skin, fell onto her face to mix with the quick tears that tumbled to her cheeks from the devastation she'd handed to her husband, but all she wanted to do was to have Kip safely back with her. Then she could apologize and grovel in front of Thomas in the hopes that he would forgive her.

Another round of barking echoed in the nighttime air.

She wheeled about toward the street with her heartbeat ticking so fast she feared her heart might explode. Since it was nearly midnight and church services would occur soon, a fair bit of traffic occupied the area. "Oh, please don't go into the street."

"Olivia, wait!"

Ignoring Thomas' shout, she continued to run, following the sound of the barks, and then her world seemed to go in slow motion. There was a flash of rusty fur and jaunty tail in the darkened street, and just as the dog entered the thoroughfare to cross and reach her side, a carriage tore down the street at high speed, the driver of which sat tilted in his seat with his chin nearly to his chest. He was either sleepy or drunk, but it didn't matter, for he wasn't paying attention, and at the breakneck speed in which he traveled as well as swerving back and forth in the lane, he would soon hit her dog.

"Kip!" She didn't think, she just reacted. The poor Pomeranian had reached the middle of the road, saw the carriage, and he froze, his little body shaking. Somewhere in the distance, she heard another shout from the viscount—or rather his urgent cry of warning as it were—but she physically threw herself into the street in front of the oncoming horse and carriage. Seconds later, as she hit the hardpacked earth, smelled the dirt and horse excrement, she bundled Kip into her arms and then rolled onto her side with her back facing the doom that bore down upon her in order to shield her dog from harm.

Perhaps it was better that she wouldn't see what would probably spell her death, but then she couldn't help it. Olivia glanced over her shoulder. The horse was there, rearing up on hind legs. The startled shout from the driver as the carriage thrashed and skidded into an arc. The sudden deceleration of velocity caused it to tip onto its side, but the horse that pulled it was beyond spooked. The whites of its eyes showed clearly in the flying snow. The terrified whinny blended with the driver's curses and Thomas' yells of alarm.

Then she screamed as the hooves came crashing down over her. Pain shot through her left hip, her arm on that side, her temple, as the horse continued onward and caught her beneath its hooves while it dragged the carriage behind.

As best she could, she held Kip against her chest with her arms around him, keeping him from being squished by either the hard-packed earth or the horse and vehicle. The poor thing whined with fear and the warmth on her belly from where he'd piddled on her gown seeped into an abstract section of her brain as darkness encroached upon her from the sides of her vision.

Frightened and racked with waves of pain, Olivia collapsed onto the ground with Kip held tight against her as tears fell onto her cheeks. Men shouted as they ran toward the scene.

"Olivia!"

Through the darkness and the whirling vortex that sucked at her consciousness, Thomas' terror-filled cry penetrated her brain. Tears fell faster now, for she'd destroyed her budding marriage with senseless, hurtful words said out of fear when she should have thought logically, when she knew all he'd wanted to do was help. "Thomas..."

He threw himself to his knees near her head regardless of the chaos. "I'm here, sweeting, I'm here." The coolness of his hand against her forehead was amazing. "I couldn't save Cynthia, but I'll be damned if I can't save you now." Shock lined his blanched face and concern shadowed his eyes, yet the fight to remain conscious proved too much for her.

With a whisper of sound, she gave into the darkness as the sensation of a rough and wet tongue tickled her chin.

Chapter Fifteen

December 26, 1817
Boxing Day

"What am I going to do if she doesn't wake?"

A low bark was his only response, for the only other living being in the library with him that evening was Sir Kippington-Prestwick, his wife's rust-colored Pomeranian who had more enthusiasm than sense.

"You'll be lost too, won't you?" He grunted when the dog laid a tiny paw on his thigh as they both watched the flames crackle behind the ornamental iron grate.

And through it all, he couldn't stop thinking about the events that had happened less than a day ago, the things that had started right here in this room, the words Olivia had hurled at him that had cut him deeper than anything he'd ever lived through, that hurt worse than when Cynthia had died.

That wasn't the worst of it. Every time he closed his eyes, he saw the horrible accident unfold again and again before him, and there was nothing he could do about it. Over and over, he watched in horror as his wife dove into the street to shield her dog from harm, but she'd taken the brunt of it herself. He'd had no time to dash out after her, and then there was nothing except flailing hooves, the sickening crunch of the carriage as it broke when it had tipped over, of the cries that echoed through his brain.

And then the silence that was all too acute, both in the street outside his townhouse and in the suite upstairs where his wife lay even now, unconscious.

It had been tricky indeed to extricate her from the wreckage, but he must have exhibited superhuman strength in order to get to her, for the men who had assisted had told him he'd refused to be denied. Then he'd examined her on that cold, snowy street, and when it had been determined nothing vital was broken, he'd scooped her and the dog into his arms, brought them inside and immediately upstairs to her rooms, and called for a surgeon.

It was then he'd remembered the staff had gone out for church services.

With nothing else for it, he returned to the street and enlisted the aid of a random stranger, imploring them to run to a specific address he'd quickly scrawled on a scrap of paper, with the promise of a large monetary reward once the task was complete.

An hour later, a surgeon had exited the room, rather grumpy to be missing his dinner, and told Thomas that Olivia suffered from a concussion. She would eventually wake on her own, but until that time, it was anyone's guess what the state of her mind was. Also, she suffered a rather large bruise on her left hip and strained muscles in her left arm where she'd shielded the dog from the horse's hooves, but there were no broken bones, and she wasn't in immediate danger.

After that, there had been nothing to do except sit by her bedside, make her as comfortable as he could, and then explain to the staff when they'd returned from church.

Now, almost a full day later, a somber pall had fallen over his house, for the servants somehow blamed him for seeing the woman they doted on lying in bed suffering a concussion. With a sigh, he scratched Kip behind the ears. The firelight reflected on the pair of scissors he'd retrieved from the garden earlier that day when he'd taken the dog out. Impressive workmanship to disguise a knife with a pair of scissors. An ache had set up around his heart since the accident flared, and he wished she were here in the room with him, threatening him with the weapon as she'd done a few times before.

Then he noticed bright red wool sticking out from beneath a pillow on the sofa. "What's this?" he asked the dog, and not receiving an answer—of course—Thomas tugged it out. A tidy muffler had been folded and hidden. A scrap of paper and a pencil nub were nestled in one of the folds, and the paper had "Thomas" scrawled across it, with an incomplete message beneath only showing an "I…"

Oh, God. She probably hadn't the time to finish the sentiment for they'd had that horrid disagreement shortly after they'd returned from Pennington's dinner. The words she'd hurled at him had sounded quite final, but he hoped she'd only said them out of anger or uncertainty surrounding the whereabouts of Kip.

With a wad of unshed tears stuck in his throat, he brought the muffler to his nose. It smelled like lilacs—like her. And to think she'd sat here knitting this for him all those hours he'd read poetry to her, or they'd discussed topics of interest to them both, knowing that she would gift it to him on Christmas, but due to a quirk of fate, they had missed the holiday.

"I need her, Kip," he whispered to the dog, who pricked his ears, and he grinned like a fool. What sort of things had Olivia said to the canine about him? "She is exactly what I've been searching for all these years, what I'd hoped to have in Cynthia. She is who I must have beside me if I'm to be effective in society, to help me be the man I should have been all those years ago." Trying not to concentrate on his aching heart, he looped the muffler about his neck in a poor attempt to have his wife close. "There must be something we can do."

The sound of running feet echoed along the corridor and abruptly stopped at the door to the library. Then Wallace darted into the room with his white hair in disarray and his eyes wild. "My lord, you must come."

Thomas slowly stood as Kip bounded to a pillow. They both stared at the butler. "What is amiss, Wallace?"

"Lady Ashbury is awake," he said in a voice that was both hushed and ramped with excitement. "She is a bit disoriented and bruised, but otherwise well, according to her maid."

"What?" He grabbed the back of the sofa for no other reason than to stay upright. "Olivia is awake?" His knees were far too weak to stand so he sat down abruptly on the sofa and displaced Kip, who uttered a sharp bark in rebuke.

"She is, my lord, and her maid said she wants to see you."

Relief shot through his chest. "She remembers me."

"So it seems." Wallace raised an eyebrow. "Shall I tell her you'll come or—"

"I will go up directly," he said as he once more shot to his feet. "Come, Kip. Let's go see your mistress." *And hope to God she still wants to be my wife.* It was pure insanity how livid he was when he'd learned she'd name a dog after him, but now said canine was nearly a constant companion. Still racked by shock and relief, he hugged the butler as he passed. "It is a miracle, my good man."

"Indeed it is, my lord," the older man said with amusement lining his face as he took in the bright red muffler about Thomas' neck. "I will spread the good news to the rest of the staff."

"Tell it far and wide." But apprehension tied his gut into knots, for he had no idea what his reception would be after the words that were exchanged. He took the stairs two treads at a time, but when he reached the door to her suite, he paused, drew a deep breath, and let it ease out as he regarded the dog. "Let us hope for the best, hmm?"

Kip yapped in agreement.

Slowly, Thomas pressed the door latch and then equally slowly he pushed open the wooden panel. Because he entered her suite by way of the door to Olivia's bedchamber, the first thing he saw was his wife sitting propped up in the four-poster bed with a bevy of pillows at her back. Strips of linen had been wrapped about her head, no doubt to stem the flow of blood from the cut at her temple, while her left arm was held in a makeshift sling made from one of his cravats. A shift and a shawl covered her top half while the rest of her was hidden beneath the bedclothes. Glad to see her upright and as alert as she could be, he swept his gaze over her person to reassure himself she was well.

Kip, wildly excited to see her again, went round and round in tight circles in front of the bed until Thomas picked him up, then deposited the dog on the bed. He immediately scampered over the bedclothes to squirm into Olivia's lap, climb up her chest, and lick any portion of herself he could come into contact with.

"Oh, Kip, I'm so glad to see you." Though she spoke to the dog, her clear gray gaze rested squarely on Thomas. "It doesn't look like you were harmed."

The sound of her voice was like a balm to his spirit, and as he took in the red tresses that spilled over her shoulders in a tangled mess, caught sight of the wash of golden freckles on her pale face, he fought with the emotion climbing his throat. "He has acted like he always has," he finally said, and the words sounded all too graveled. "Hasn't left my side since the accident."

She nodded. In the candlelight, bruising was evident on the left side of her face. "Is it Christmas?" Her gaze fell on the cheerful muffler about his neck. "You found your gift."

The poor dear. "No, Christmas was yesterday. I'm afraid you passed it while unconscious. Today is Boxing Day, but yes. I found the muffler shortly before being told that you were awake." He touched the garment with a hand, but there was so much left unsaid stuck in his throat, waiting on the tip of his tongue. "Thank you. It's the most meaningful gift I have ever been given." Truly, he would treasure it for the rest of his life.

"I thought you might look dapper with a splash of color near to your face, and it will help keep the chill away." Her voice was a tad weak and scratchy. When she reached for a cut crystal glass of water that rested on her bedside table, her hand shook.

"It's wonderful." *Like you.* "Uh, what is the last thing you remember?" That wasn't what he wanted to discuss, but it was needed to assess the state of her mind.

Her lips pushed into a frown after she'd taken a few sips of water and replaced the glass. "There are flashes, pictures in my head of a rearing horse, a carriage approaching all too quickly." She touched her immobile left arm with the fingers of her right. "I remember falling to the ground, but then there is nothing. Only a curious... emptiness between that moment and now." When she attempted a shrug, a wince of pain went over her face. "I assume I acquired the injuries during the accident?"

"You did." Not wishing to have such a wide gulf of space between them, Thomas went to her bedside and slipped into the plain wooden chair there. Kip, with his affections clearly divided, trotted over the bed between them, almost as if he were pacing. As succinctly as possible, Thomas relayed what had happened from his point of view, and in the telling of the story, he again relived every horrid moment. "You were so still while lying in the street as people gathered around. I thought in that moment I had truly lost you." He cleared his throat, for though the words were difficult, they had to be said. "Everything went terribly clear in that one moment suspended in time. I knew without any doubts that I loved you, but I also feared that it didn't matter, after what you'd said to me in the library..."

"Oh, Thomas. I am so sorry."

"I apologize for what I said. Kip is more than merely a dog," he said in a ragged whisper as she ruffled the canine's fur with one hand.

"He is, but he is no more important than anyone else, you included." Concern and grief clouded her eyes. A wash of embarrassment went through her expression. "I didn't mean those words I said in the library. They were borne out of fear, said in the heat of anger when I fell back on old habits, when I thought I would lose yet another member of my circle unexpectedly." The delicate tendons of her throat worked with a hard swallow. "I immediately regretted them as soon as I said them."

Christ, but hearing that was much like a benediction from the heavenly host or a pardon to a man with a noose about his neck. He rubbed a hand along the side of his face, and when he looked at her, he couldn't help the moisture welling in his eyes. "That makes my heart glad."

Answering tears sprang to her eyes. Kip, apparently bored, settled into a ball on her lap. "Did you mean what you said earlier?"

"It has been a trying handful of days, sweeting. You will have to help me remember." The endearment slipped out as if it were the most natural thing, and he hoped he would have the right to always call her that.

Her giggle fell flat. A tear slipped down her cheek. "That you love me."

"Ah." Leaning forward, he took her good hand, threaded their fingers together. "Yes, it is true." He paused as he peered into her eyes, and he didn't care that tears slid to his own cheeks. Now was not the time to deny emotion. Sometimes, the people closest in one's life needed to see how their presence affected others, how much they truly meant. "I have been running away from feeling anything, from letting myself acknowledge emotions for seven years since Cynthia died and my world shifted." After he'd forced a hard swallow into his suddenly dry throat, he continued, "I don't want to run any longer."

Olivia's eyes rounded. She clung to his hand. "That is wonderful to hear, but why? What happened to make you completely change everything?"

What happened, indeed. He offered a slow grin and was rewarded by a blush on her cheeks. "You." Quite simply, that was the reason. "My world shifted again when you came into it." His voice wavered. "When I thought I would lose you that horrible night beneath the wild horse and broken carriage, I just stopped fighting everything and let myself complete the fall which started the first damned time you put the tip of your blade to my throat. It might be too fast, but I rather don't think love cares about that."

"Truly, I thought I wanted to kill you." A half-stifled sob escaped her as she wiped at the moisture on her cheeks. "I don't any longer, if you wondered."

He kissed the back of her hand. "A lovely sentiment, especially as I hope to remain at your side for a long while yet."

"Oh?"

"Very much so." Though she hadn't told him how she felt about him, he could no longer keep mum on the words he needed to say. "It is time for the truth to come out. Yes, I fought against marrying you because I assumed it would have been a betrayal of Cynthia's memory, but as the week went on and I came to know you, understand you, I realized what you and I have between us was much different from that long-ago love."

To her credit, Olivia didn't interrupt. Silent tears trickled to her cheeks while Kip dozed in her lap. With the strips of linen about her head and her arm in a sling, she was far too vulnerable, and the urge to protect her grew.

"Yes, I loved Cynthia, but it was an immature relationship. I liked that she'd been enamored with me, thought I was the greatest thing in her world. For my part, I was taken in by her beauty, by the forbidden relationship, distracted by making my father angry for yet another scandal, but once things became all too real with the pregnancy and the secret engagement, fear crept in, laid its claws into me from the moment she died and hasn't let go. I have been struggling with guilt since then."

"It wasn't your fault. Her death isn't on your hands." She squeezed his fingers. "Scandal takes two people to indulge in it, and sometimes fate isn't kind. It's time for you to come out of that prison who've made for yourself."

"Agreed, and that has happened over the course of the week with you. I'm beginning to see those events quite differently, and though she will always exist in my memories, my heart has now been released and cleansed so that it has room to usher in a new love."

"And?" she asked in a breathless voice.

Thomas shrugged. "I didn't fall in love with you, Olivia. I walked into that love with my eyes wide open. I chose to take every step along the way, even when my heart disagreed with my head, and in such a short time to boot." He brushed the pad of his thumb over her knuckles. "I believe in fate; it hasn't been kind to either of us. However, I also believe we are only fated to do the things we would have chosen anyway." When his voice broke, he ignored that tell of emotion. "Sweeting, I would choose you, in a hundred ways, a hundred lifetimes, again and again. I would choose you because I love you. There is nothing else to say."

Her eyes were gorgeous and luminous with moisture. "That is the most romantic thing any man has ever said to me."

He snorted. "I have my moments."

Using a portion of the sheet, she mopped the tears from her face and winced since she'd moved her left arm to do so. Her right hand shook in his. "You are obviously more gifted with words when you choose to use them, and that is something I can never match you with, but I knew I was falling in love with you the afternoon we sat in Hyde Park and watched your daughter feed the swans. After coming to know your caring and compassionate heart, exploring the pain you've hidden behind, learning what type of man you let people see when your guard is down, that love is only growing." That sentiment was reflected in the gray depths of her eyes, and he feared he might drown in it.

"I can only be who I am," he said in a soft voice as his chin trembled. "I have hidden that man for so long beneath vices and grief, that not doing so feels a bit odd."

"It will be easier as time goes on, but I understand. I am working on that as well... as evidenced by what I said to you when Kip was lost."

"Hush. That is in the past."

"Thank you." Her smile was a watery affair, but she had never been more dear to him. "I can't wait to see how our union will grow."

"Neither can I, which has made me wish to start over."

"How so?"

"Olivia Rose Prestwick, will you marry me again?"

"What?" Confusion filled her expression. "We were already wed, nearly ten days ago."

"I know that, but said nuptial ceremony rested upon a foundation of anger, revenge, guilt, and grief. For our marriage to succeed, I want to marry you again, and this time for the right reasons. Will you agree?"

For long moments she regarded him, then she nodded. "I cannot wait to be your wife in all the ways that matter." When she brought his hand to her lips, she kissed his palm and curled his fingers over it. "I also want to bear your children, give you an heir, regardless of the risk, but promise me that if one of them is like Sally, we will never send them away or forget them."

His heart squeezed. Truly, she was everything he needed. "I promise. Family is family and should be together." Then he leaned into her and pressed his lips to hers in a gentle kiss. Not wishing to jostle her by sharing a full embrace, he merely wanted to show her the depth of his feelings. All too soon, he pulled away. "I am going to let you rest and heal, for I have plans to attend and guests to notify."

"Will you come back soon?"

"Nothing could keep me away." Needing to touch her again, he dropped a kiss to her forehead. "And don't let Sir Kippington boss you. Since he survived the accident, he truly does think he's invincible and that everyone should worship him." His lips twitched when she chuckled. "But he's a good boy."

This time, when he left her room, his steps were light and his heart full. Life was a series of peaks and valleys. It was lovely, then horrid, then lovely again. The trick was not being afraid to continue onward, for one season wouldn't remain for long.

Chapter Sixteen

December 31, 1817
Ashbury House
Manchester Square
London, England

"Good heavens, why am I so nervous? It's not as if this is my first time marrying the same groom," Olivia said to Lady Pennington, who fussed with how the white net overskirt lay over her gold satin gown.

"Hush. You look gorgeous and nerves are perfectly acceptable, especially when you are doing it for all the *right* reasons this time." The lady smiled, and the gesture reflected in her eyes. "The gold with the red hair is quite stunning, and if your husband doesn't find himself tongue-tied today, he is quite the nodcock." She giggled. "Also, the white rabbit fur around the bodice and hem of this gown makes it so luxurious and quite fitting to welcome in the new year."

"Apparently Ashbury thought we should leave all old business and feelings with the old year, so our new lives together aren't so cluttered." Her heart squeezed. She had no idea how romantic he was until recently, and she couldn't have enough of it.

"Isn't it interesting that the men we were forced to wed through odd wagers at the Lyon's Den are the exact men that we needed all along?"

Olivia snorted. She leaned close to the countess. "Don't let Mrs. Dove-Lyon hear you say that, else she'll be relentless with her unofficial matchmaking."

They both dissolved into giggles, then a low buzz of voices proceeded the men into the room, along with their intimate guest list. She smiled at the earl as well as at Captain Huxley. The same vicar who'd married them before brought up the rear. With a wave to Mr. Adamson and his young clerk, and a wide grin at her brother, she turned back to Lady Pennington. "I suppose it's time."

"It is. For many things." Joy sparkled in the countess' eyes as she took Olivia's hands in hers. "Enjoy the moment, my dear. Love is wonderful, of course, but it's not a magical elixir that will suddenly make everything blissful. You still need to work at marriage, and on occasion go toe-to-toe with your husband when the disagreements arrive."

"I know." She sobered. "Good thing I enjoy verbally bantering with Ashbury."

"That's part of the fun." With a wink, the countess moved away and then sat on a sofa next to her husband. He immediately whispered something into her ear that made her blush and giggle.

Olivia's heart fluttered, for everything was so different now that she didn't want to murder her groom. Then Wallace was at the open double-doors. He grinned at her seconds before he stood aside to reveal the viscount.

Good heavens, he is so handsome!

It had been planned that she'd come into the drawing room ahead of Thomas, but he maintained he had a surprise for her, and as she drew her gaze up and down his form, she touched the emeralds that rested around her neck. Once more he was clad in evening attire with a tailcoat, but it was the golden brocade waistcoat that tugged a smile from her. How sweet he'd wanted to match her gown. As he advanced into the room, she noticed he led Kip on a leather lead, and around the dog's neck glittered the emerald bracelet included in the parure he'd given her.

She glanced at the vicar, who looked quizzically at the dog as he joined her. "Isn't he such a darling?" she asked in a soft voice of the man.

"The viscount or the dog?"

"Exactly." Why couldn't she stop smiling? She waved to Wallace as he and a handful of servants came into the room and stood in a line at the back near the door. They had become her family since she'd become Lady Ashbury, and there was no way she wanted them left out, especially since she'd missed the Boxing Day festivities.

The older man grunted as Thomas joined them. "It is highly irregular, asking to be wed a second time to the same woman."

"Yes, well, I am not the usual man." He winked at her. "And my bride is most certainly not the usual sort of woman."

"Very well." The clergyman waved Mr. Rodgers away. "You'll need to sign the register once more afterward."

"I am more than happy to do whatever is needed, for this is quite a special day." He bumped her shoulder with his. "Good morning."

"Hullo." She hadn't seen him yet this morning, and they certainly hadn't shared a bed or anything intimate since before her accident, but now that she was well on her way to full healing, every touch, every glance from him brought awareness of him to the forefront.

The vicar cleared his throat. "Will there be any more guests?"

"I believe everyone is here who matters." Thomas glanced across the room, sent a small grin to Mrs. Dove-Lyon as she slipped into a chair toward the rear of the space away from the windows and the anemic late December sunshine. As before, she wore a bonnet with veils that covered the upper portion of her face. Her dark green gown and matching pelisse was the only concession to the waning Christmastide holidays.

With a faint huff, Mr. Adamson led them toward the fireplace, where cheerful flames danced behind a decorative iron grate. Just as before. "The nuptial couple is ready to begin, so I shouldn't keep them waiting. Even though this is quite confusing. After all, they are already wed."

A few chuckles circled about the assembled guests, but Olivia didn't begrudge them their amusement. She and Thomas were doing this for them; no one needed to know a reason.

"Lord Ashbury, Lady Ashbury, please face me." When they did, he opened his book to the appropriate page. "Dearly beloved, we are gathered together here in the sight of God, and in the face of these witnesses, to join together this Man and this Woman in holy Matrimony; which is an honorable estate, instituted of God in the time of man's innocency, signifying unto us the mystical union that is betwixt Christ and his Church…"

Olivia fairly vibrated with excitement. At her feet, Kip paced back and forth in front of her and Thomas. The emeralds sparkled amidst his fur, and it looked for all the world as if he were grinning. Never had she thought she would have grown to actually love the man standing beside her, but miracles started when two people lowered their guards and weren't afraid of appearing vulnerable to each other.

"Stop woolgathering, sweeting," he whispered against the shell of her ear. "It makes me wonder if you truly wish to wed me."

She softly scoffed and met his eyes. "There is nothing I would rather do," she said in an equally low voice.

Mr. Adamson cleared his throat then addressed Thomas. "Wilt thou have this Woman to thy wedded Wife, to live together after God's ordinance in the holy estate of Matrimony? Wilt thou love her, comfort her, honor her, and keep her in sickness and in health; and, forsaking all others, keep thee only unto her, so long as ye both shall live?"

Olivia looked at him as anticipation twisted up her spine.

"I..." He glanced between her and the vicar. "I will," he uttered and the emotion in his eyes sent frissons of need through her belly.

"Excellent," Mr. Adamson said. He put a forefinger to the words on one page as he addressed her. "Wilt thou have this Man to thy wedded Husband, to live together after God's ordinance in the holy estate of Matrimony? Wilt thou obey him, and serve him, love him, honor him, and keep him in sickness and in health; and, forsaking all others, keep thee only unto him, so long as ye both shall live?"

"I most certainly will. Now and always." She couldn't help but grin at her husband. "Though I still cannot make a promise that I will obey him, but I will certainly be open to discussing anything I don't agree with."

A few more chuckles went through the guests.

"Especially when those discussions turn into something else entirely or might even be scandalous if they were overheard."

"Do remember this *is* a holy ceremony and shouldn't be taken lightly," Mr. Adamson said as consternation lined his face. "It matters not if you are already wed to each other. I refuse to have you make jest of this holy estate." He then instructed Thomas to take her right hand in his right, which he then did. Olivia's hand trembled. "Lord Ashbury, please repeat after me..."

Thomas grinned, and there was a wicked light in his eyes. "I will, of course, but if you will allow me a moment to say a few of my own words, Mr. Adamson?"

The clergyman frowned. "This is most irregular, but I don't suppose there is anything *wrong* with it..."

"Ah, thank you." He turned fully to her and held both of her hands in his while he met her gaze. "Olivia, you have been the most surprising, the most maddening, the most confusing, and the most exciting addition to my life."

A tiny sigh escaped her. "As you said days ago, I can only be who I am."

"Indeed." For the space of a few heartbeats, he was silent, perhaps wishing to order his words. "Since the day you and I were first wed, I knew you would challenge me. What I didn't know was that you would try to stab me on our wedding night, but somehow, that event seemed to wake me from the doze I'd fallen into." His voice wavered. "Over the course of our union, I have had cause to examine the man I wish to be, in large part because you wouldn't let me hide in the past." His chin trembled. "We have both grown so much in the short time we have had together. It's safe to say you enrich my life and inspire me to be a better man—for us both."

"Oh, Thomas!" She squeezed his fingers as tears sprang to her eyes. "How lovely."

"I am not quite finished, sweeting." He winked. "I promise to love you and always be by your side, through everything that fate should give us."

Olivia swallowed around the ball of tears in her throat. "I vow to always be faithful, and always be your constant companion, and perhaps the voice of reason, no matter what the future might bring." If they were blessed with children who were not quite the best mentally, she would love them still and nurture them with all the love she could. The children would be a part of her and a part of him. No one would be sent away.

He held fast to her hands. "I promise to support you in whatever dreams you have or however you wish to change and challenge our world."

Butterflies danced through her belly, for she would soon tell him of her desire to open a business that might match childless couples who wished to be parents with unwanted children. "I promise to love and support you no matter where life takes us."

By increments, he leaned closer to her. "I promise to spend the rest of my days loving you madly and well so you should harbor no doubts."

"Oh!" A tear slipped to her cheek. "I promise to cherish you for the rest of your life, for there is no one else for me better than you."

A soft sound of sniffling echoed in the room, no doubt belonging to the countess.

Mr. Adamson harrumphed. "If I could continue, Lord Ashbury?" When Thomas nodded, the vicar said, "Please repeat after me."

With a grin that had tiny fires erupting in her blood, Thomas did as instructed. "I, Thomas Charles Prestwick, Viscount of Ashbury, take thee Olivia Rose Prestwick, Viscountess of Ashbury, as my wedded Wife—again—to have and to hold from this day forward, for better for worse, for richer for poorer, in sickness and in health, to love and to cherish, until death us do part..." His voice wavered. Clearly, this was quite an emotional time for him. "... according to God's holy ordinance; and thereto I plight thee my troth."

Mr. Adamson nodded. "Please release hands. Lord Ashbury, take her left in yours."

Once they'd done as instructed, Mr. Adamson trained his attention on Olivia. "Lady Ashbury, repeat after me." He gave her the words, much like the ones he'd said to Thomas moments before.

With another quick glance at her husband and catching his nod of encouragement, she smiled. "I, Olivia Rose Prestwick, Viscountess of Ashbury, take thee Thomas Charles Prestwick, Viscount of Ashbury, as my wedded Husband—again, and correctly this time." Her voice broke on the last word. "And I will do so for as many times as it will take until you believe you are worthy of a lasting love. To have and to hold from this day forward, for better for worse, for richer for poorer, in sickness and in health, to love, cherish, and to obey, until death us do part, according to God's holy ordinance." A sound that was much like a choked sob came from her and she once more connected her gaze with Thomas'. "And thereto I give thee my troth. I love you."

"I love you as well," the viscount whispered as his attention dropped to her mouth.

Mr. Adamson snorted. Apparently, joining an already married couple in marriage was quite annoying the second time around. "Please release your hands." To Thomas, he whispered, "You needn't give forth the ring. We have already done that, but I do expect to be paid."

"Of course. However, this is where we depart again from tradition." He dug a small leather pouch of coins from his waistcoat pocket, which he gave to the vicar, who rested it upon his open *Book of Common Prayer*. Thomas then kneeled briefly before Kip, untied something from the bejeweled collar, stood, and rested a plain silver band upon the vicar's book. "There is a ring after all."

Olivia stared with openmouthed astonishment, for that was the band he'd worn around his neck on a cord, the one he would have given Cynthia.

"Very well." Mr. Adamson murmured a few words, no doubt as a blessing, before returning the ring to him. "You may present the ring to the lady as you have planned."

Thomas held up the thin silver band. "This not only represents my past but also our shared grief over a woman who brought us together. While I have learned it's important not to let myself be lost in the past, I also think it's important to carry a few memories into our future, so that those we love will never be forgotten." So saying, he gently tugged the glove from her right hand. "If you agree?"

"How sweet you are, and you are also wise. I would be honored to wear it for a time." After all, she didn't want Cynthia's ghost to have a chance to come between them. "Until you find another ring to replace it."

"Agreed."

As soon as Thomas slipped it onto the fourth finger of her right hand, the vicar spoke again, the words directed to him. "Please repeat after me."

"With this Ring I thee wed, with my Body I thee worship, and with all my worldly Goods I thee endow. In the Name of the Father, and of the Son, and of the Holy Ghost. Amen." Again, he leaned close and fit his lips to the shell of her ear. "I cannot wait to worship your body with mine."

"Oh, goodness." Heat seeped into her cheeks. At her feet, Kip yapped as if he agreed with the second marriage and his temporary collar.

Mr. Adamson frowned. Clearly, they were far too scandalous this morning. "Please kneel while we all pray together."

Thomas kneeled while the vicar uttered his prayer, and when her arm brushed his sleeve as she did the same beside him, need shivered down her spine. He was her greatest adventure and biggest challenge, but he was also her greatest strength. With him by her side, she could do anything she put her mind to, and change the world—or at least London.

Mr. Adamson closed his book. "I now pronounce thee husband and wife. Again."

Scattered applause broke out among the gathered guests as they both rose to their feet.

"If you'll please see my clerk to sign the register, then everything will be official," the vicar said with a slight grin. "And frankly, Lord Ashbury, I do not wish to marry you a third time. These marital bonds are quite unbreakable."

"Thank God for that." Thomas glanced at her. "I don't mind being in the parson's mousetrap after all, but I will once more go against tradition this final time before we sign the register." Before Olivia knew what was happening, he tugged her into his arms, fit his lips to hers, and then proceeded to kiss her quite deeply and thoroughly until her head swam and the only thought she had was dragging him upstairs and taking him to bed.

Gasps circled through the room, quickly followed by hoots from the men present.

Eventually, Thomas released her. He winked at the vicar, who left their company with a huff, but when he looked at her, his grin was wide, and amusement danced in his eyes. "Did you think that now we're married we should give up scandal?"

"I think we should rather encourage it. Who knows? Perhaps kissing after saying vows will catch on." How much did she love this man? "Since the wedding breakfast is being hosted by the Earl of Pennington and we'll stay to ring in the new year, would it be bad form to slip away and consummate our union?" she said in a low voice for his ears alone.

"That is a fine idea." He uttered a growl as he snaked an arm about her waist. "Who knew that a game of faro would have handed me the secret dream of my heart?"

Olivia giggled. "Must have been a very lucky hand indeed." Movement across the room caught her eye. Mrs. Dove-Lyon walked toward the door, but when their gazes connected, Olivia raised a hand. The other woman nodded and then she was gone. "Or perhaps Mrs. Dove-Lyon truly is a matchmaker of some skill…"

"Perish the thought." Then he cajoled her into his arms once more and kissed her as if he had nothing to do with his time except that.

Not that she minded. After all the disappointments and sorrow fate had handed her, she couldn't wait to bask in love and follow the new paths opening up before her.

Thank you, Cynthia. I'll take care of him now. Go enjoy your eternal rest.

New beginnings were something to savor.

Epilogue

December 20, 1821
Prestwick Hall
Essex, England

THOMAS GRINNED FROM his position at the bottom of a hill near the rear of his property. He and his family had been in the countryside for little more than a week before a bout of bad weather had come in, bringing periods of heavy snow until the ground was easily covered in several inches before the skies finally cleared.

Now, everyone had been more than ready to get out of the house for a bit, so they'd all bundled up into their warmest clothing and went trekking through the snow to the hilly section of the property. There, they met with some of the tenant farmers as well as their children, who had immediately thrown themselves into the task of sledding down the hills.

"You can go down two more times, then we need to head back," he yelled up to the top where his two children were arranging themselves on the wooden sled under the watchful eye of a footman. "Your fingers and toes must be freezing."

I know mine are.

"Papa, watch us!" The command by his almost four-year-old son—Cecil—made him grin, but the trill of laughter that followed by Cecil's twin sister Charlotte had his heart squeezing. Then his stomach bottomed out as the footman gave the sled and its precious cargo a push. The children came whizzing down the gentle hill with another sled beside theirs.

At the bottom, the sled tipped over and the children spilled out. More laughter followed, then seconds later, Cecil jumped to his feet and patiently and gallantly assisted his sister to hers, for she was always a tiny bit slower and sometimes didn't understand why things ended like they did. Though they were twins and Cecil older by two minutes, Charlotte had been born with the same characteristics as both Thomas' brother as well as the daughter he'd given up for adoption years ago. But she was the dearest child he'd ever seen, full of happiness, laughter, and as great determination as her mother possessed.

"I appreciate how much you help your sister," he told his son as he brushed the worst of the snow from the lad's jacket. "You show courage and compassion. I'm proud of you."

The little boy looked up at him with pleasure in his brown eyes, and beneath his cap, wisps of red hair peeked out. "I love Charlotte." He shrugged as if that explained everything, then he gave a little hop. "One more time?"

How could Thomas deny the cherubs anything? "One more time." He glanced at the footman, who'd walked down the hill and nodded. "They want one more go 'round then we are going to home to hot tea and a fire."

"I appreciate that, my lord." But the footman grinned when Charlotte caught hold of his gloved hand and tried to tug him up the hill. She was quite bossy when she wanted to be.

With a wave, Cecil dragged the sled behind him as best he could by a bit of rope before the footman stepped in to help.

"You can relax, you know."

He turned his head at the sound of Olivia's voice. "I cannot help but worry over them. We've been out here for three hours, and already I fear appendages will start to freeze off." His breath clouded about his head in the cold, but the sun was shining, and the sky was blue. Above all, the children were enjoying themselves.

"They are young and probably don't feel the cold like older people do." She approached slowly, for she was with child again, five months along. When his wife reached his side, he immediately put an arm about her waist and leaned into her warmth. "I will be glad you are all back home. I worry too."

Damnation, but he was so incredibly fortunate. Some days he was in awe of his life, so he made certain he remained grateful for everything he'd been given.

She plucked at the red muffler he'd wound about his neck and tucked beneath his greatcoat. "I can't believe you have kept this so long."

"Why not? You made it for me, and it reminds me to never take anything for granted." But he grinned. "It's a favorite piece and I will wear it until it falls apart."

"Then I'll simply have to knit you another one." Olivia glanced up the hill. When Cecil waved, she returned the gesture. "They are growing up so fast." She sighed, and he felt that all the way to his toes.

"They are, but take heart. We'll soon have a new babe about the house to share our lives with." He still couldn't believe he had been granted such a boon, for they'd lost two infants between the twins' birth and the pregnancy Olivia carried.

"I can hardly wait. Our family is already so dear." When she turned to him, a faint frown pulled down the corners of her lips. "However, once this one is born, I think we should make efforts to prevent further pregnancies. It is too hard on my heart when things go wrong, and I grow weary of continually losing loved ones."

"Of course." He swallowed around the sudden lump in his throat. "I'll secure the proper sheaths and other things we will need, and I completely understand. There is only so much sadness a person can endure." And he would do anything to shield his wife from that. "I'm happy we have the twins and the new one. I need nothing else in my life to keep me in such a state. Besides, you have an adoption clinic to concentrate on." It was slated to open next year out of their townhouse in London. Small to start, but he had no doubt with his wife's determination, it would flourish.

"We certainly have had a few surprises since we married."

"The first or second time?" he couldn't help but quip.

"Hush, you." Yet a slow grin curved her lips, and he couldn't wait until they were home so he could kiss her. "I wouldn't have it any other way though."

Then a shout echoed down from the top of the hill. Twin giggles followed as the sled came shooting toward them, gliding effortlessly on the runners through the snow. As before, at the bottom, the children toppled over to another round of laughter.

Thomas exchanged an amused glance with Olivia. "Thank you."

"For what?" she asked as she plucked Charlotte up and brushed her off.

"For giving me all of this." He gestured about to include their whole life. "For sharing with me, for choosing to understand why I was that angry, bitter man all those years ago." As he picked Cecil up and propped him on a hip, he smiled at his wife. "For making me better so I would be ready to be the father my children would need."

"Oh." Tears welled in her eyes, but then, she'd been emotional of late due to the pregnancy. "That is so sweet, but you did the same for me. Perhaps we rescued each other."

"Perhaps we did." When Cecil squirmed, Thomas set him on his feet, and the lad took off running with Charlotte's hand in his. They followed the footman who carried the sled. Her little bonnet slipped off to hang at her back, and her glorious red curls ran riot about her head. Truly, she was her mother's daughter, and he adored them both. "I've been thinking."

"Didn't you once tell me that was a horrible thing for a man to do?" Teasing sparkled in her luminous eyes.

"I did, but I no longer believe that." He linked his arm with hers, to provide support as she navigated the snow more than anything else. "In any event, since we lost our dear Sir Kippington last winter, I want to give the children a puppy for Christmas this year, but only if you are in agreement."

Laughter escaped her, and he reveled in the sound. "That's a wonderful idea. I have missed having the patter of doggie feet in the house."

"Good. One of the farmers has a dog with a litter of puppies that will be ready for adoption by next week. Dear little beagle pups that will have enough energy to keep up with the twins."

"And will give me a bit of a reprieve." She nodded. "You are a good man, Thomas."

It made him feel that he could do anything every time she praised him. "I am only doing my best, but thank you." With a quick glance about and seeing no one near enough to cry scandal, he halted, tugged her into his arms, and claimed her cold lips in a slow but sensual kiss designed to tease. Just as quickly, he pulled away and resumed walking toward the manor. "Once the children are asleep tonight, perhaps you and I should retire."

A faint blush stained her freckled cheeks, and he loved her all the more for it, even after all this time. "What a lovely idea. It's been a bit since we've had time alone, and our anniversary is coming up soon. I might need you to remind me that I made the right choice by marrying you twice."

"I look forward to it." He glanced ahead at their twins, and he couldn't help another grin. Yes, life was quite amazing when it came down to brass tacks. That didn't mean there weren't heartbreaks, sorrows, or misunderstandings. It simply meant that instead of running away from those things, he'd chosen to talk about them and walk through those troubles with the best person for him by his side. There was nothing wrong with growing as a person and making the needed and necessary changes to live his best life.

And in that, he'd finally found his redemption.

The End

About the Author

Sign up for Sandra's bi-monthly newsletter and you'll be given exclusive excerpts, cover reveals before the general public as well as opportunities to enter contests you won't find anywhere else.

Just send an email to sandrasookoo@yahoo.com with SUBSCRIBE in the subject line.

Or follow/friend her on social media:
Facebook: facebook.com/sandra.sookoo
Facebook Author Page: facebook.com/sandrasookooauthor
Pinterest: pinterest.com/sandrasookoo
Instagram: instagram.com/sandrasookoo
BookBub Page: bookbub.com/authors/sandra-sookoo

Made in United States
Troutdale, OR
10/30/2023

14150611R00122